⊕RIGINALS

NEW WRITING FROM
BRITAIN'S OLDEST PUBLISHER

This is the second year of JM Originals,
a list from John Murray.
It is a home for fresh and distinctive new writing;
for books that provoke and entertain.

The Bed Moved

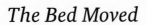

The Bed Moved

STORIES

Rebecca Schiff

JM ORIGINALS

First published in Great Britain in 2016 by JM Originals
An imprint of John Murray (Publishers)
An Hachette UK Company

1

© Rebecca Schiff 2016

The right of Rebecca Schiff to be identified as the Author of the Work
has been asserted by her in accordance with the Copyright, Designs
and Patents Act 1988.

A CIP catalogue record for this title is available from the British Library

Trade Paperback ISBN 978-1-47363-184-7
Ebook ISBN 978-1-47363-185-4

The following stories first appeared in these publications:
The American Reader: "http://www.msjiz/boxx374/mpeg" published as
"Boxing Experiment A38" (October 2014)
Electric Literature: "It Doesn't Have to Be a Big Deal" (December 4, 2013)
Fence: "Another Cake" (Spring/Summer 2010)
Guernica: "F = ma" (July 1, 2007)
n+1: "The Bed Moved" (Spring 2006), "Men Against Violence" (December 14,
2012), "My Allergies Will Charm You" published as "Pick a Fish" (Spring 2006),
and "Welcome Lilah" (Spring 2006)

Printed and bound by CPI Group (UK) Ltd, Croydon, CR0 4YY

John Murray policy is to use papers that are natural, renewable and
recyclable products and made from wood grown in sustainable forests.
The logging and manufacturing processes are expected to conform to
the environmental regulations of the country of origin.

John Murray (Publishers)
Carmelite House
50 Victoria Embankment
London EC4Y 0DZ

www.johnmurray.co.uk

For my mother

Contents

Contents

The Bed Moved

The Bed Moved

THERE WERE film majors in my bed—they talked about film. There were poets, coxswains, guys trying to grow beards.

"Kids get really scared when their dad grows a beard," I said.

Finally, I had an audience. I helped a pitcher understand the implications of his team's hazing ritual. I encouraged indecisive dancer-anthropologists to double major. When a guy apologized for being sweaty, I got him a small towel. I made people feel good.

Then I took a break. Then I forgot that I was taking a break. Spring was here. Jake was here. Also Josh. One dancer-anthropologist dropped anthropology, just did dance. He danced with honors.

"Mazel tov," I said.

The bed moved. Movers moved it. Movers asked what my dad did, why he wasn't moving the bed.

New guys came to the bed. New guys had been in the Gulf War, had been bisexual, had taken out teeth, had taken out ads. Musical types left CDs with their names markered on—I kept a pile. I was careful not to smudge them, scratch them. (Scratch that, I wasn't careful.)

"So many musicians in this city," I observed, topless.

Boxer shorts were like laundry even on their bodies. Guys burrowed down for not long enough, popped up, smiled.

Did I have something? Did I have anything?

I did.

Something, anything, went in the trash, except one, which didn't. One hadn't gone on in the first place.

After, cell phones jingled: Be Bop, Mariachi Medley, Chicken Dance, Die Alone.

Nervous, I felt nervous. There was mariachi in the trains, or else it was just one guy playing "La Bamba." I slow-danced into clinic waiting rooms. Receptionists told me to relax and try to enjoy the weekend, since we wouldn't know anything till Monday. Sunday I lost it, banged my face against the bed. Be easy, girl, I thought. Be bop. Something was definitely wrong with me—I never called myself "girl." I played CDs, but CDs by artists who had already succeeded. They had succeeded for a reason. They weren't wasting time in my bed. One did pass through the bed, to brag. He had been divorced, had met Madonna.

He asked, "Is this what women are like now?"

Longviewers

MOMMY AND DADDY hate the other street. The other street used to be just another street, but now it wants to give us its traffic, to cause us pain. Now Mommy and Daddy host meetings in our house like it is union times. If it were union times, we wouldn't have a house, or artichoke appetizers for the other angry people, but the spirit would be the same. I've never seen Mommy and Daddy so worked up. Usually, they're at work. They just go to work and they hardly have friends. Not like me, who's always on the phone, dampening the little holes. They got me Line 2, and when it's for me, they yell, "Line 2!" like it's my name. I never even noticed the traffic on our street. I don't even drive.

"You still call them that?" says Kira, a friend who also has her own line. "I stopped calling my parents Mommy and Daddy when I learned to tie my shoes."

"You're so mature," I say. "Can you give me maturity lessons?"

Daddy tells me to get off the phone, it's time for Save-Our-Street strategy.

Daddy, he's incensed about the other street, his neck bull-frogging out over his tie. He's not even loosening the tie anymore, just gets home from work and starts dialing his new friends, Bruce and Bruce, the other save-the-street fanatics. Daddy's got a widower friend now, too, and the never-married Vietnamese woman with a Long Island accent who gardens. She plants bulbs, waves him over for the update.

"They've got a lawyer now," she hisses, smushing dirt.

"That's okay," he says. "We've got the mafia."

Daddy jokes, but only with our street. With the other street, he makes a point of racing down it, pounding the horn. He goes to town meetings and curses the mayor, whose name is May Hamburger. May Hamburger is in somebody's pocket on the other street. They claim their street, Longview, is too narrow to have two-way traffic. Last spring, they say, a child almost died. Our street, Hillview, is wider; a thoroughfare, a boulevard. Hillview can accommodate.

But Mommy says they're just worried about property values. The Longviewers, she says, only care about money.

"That kid did need stitches," I say.

"Longviewers are selfish. They could care less if we live or if we die." She's folding chairs.

"How much did our house cost?" I ask.

"A lot," says Daddy.

"It's about safety," she says, plunking a chair against a chair. "It's about not getting stepped on. You know, the Longviewers hired a lawyer."

"This is like the Balkans," I say. "This is how ethnic conflict gets started."

We did ethnic conflict last year in Integrated Studies, which is English and Social Studies combined in a classroom with an accordion divider. This year, we're reading our thirty-seventh Steinbeck and getting quizzed on kamikaze pilots. Did they:

A) Drop an atomic bomb on Hiroshima?
B) Fly on wind power alone?
C) Undertake suicide missions on behalf of the Japanese government during World War II?
D) Strafe Longview?

At least we're not learning about Helen Keller anymore. Sometimes I write invisible letters on Kira's hand in Integrated Studies. T-H-I-S (flat palm) S-U-C-K-S. We're not making fun of Helen Keller, just using her techniques to get by. We have our own handicaps. Boys who crack Helen Keller jokes ignore our collective lack of breast. They're probably from Longview.

No, Kira doesn't live on the other street. She's just a friend from the town. Kira thinks my parents are "awesome." Once, I think, she saw them kissing.

AWESOME DADDY is now shouting "Furthermore" into a tape recorder.

"He's losing it," says Mommy, not at all scared.

Did he ever have it? I really don't know. In the photo albums, he looks peaceful, with a fatter tie. The albums are pre-me. Mommy and Daddy slide around under loose plastic flaps, in front of trolley cars, the Dead Sea. Maybe trolley cars are the answer to the problems of street. Maybe monorail. In Technology, we cut out articles about electric cars, then paste the articles onto paper a little bigger than the articles. Electric-car articles hang around the room, next to articles about Maglev trains.

Kira and I sand a lot in Technology. Our bridges are almost soft. But hers, with tighter scaffolding and a two-pyramid base, holds more pebbles. My bridge is not strong. I keep working on it. It keeps breaking. I keep fixing it. The bridge project is a way to pass the quarter until it is time for the end of wood. Then we have Math. Math seems to be about fractions canceling each other out, about objects in space, and the cute fish of infinity.

"Furthermore," Daddy repeats, almost kissing the tape recorder. "Furthermore, if the town chooses to make Longview Road a one-way street without a fair hearing, then we, the residents of Hillview Road, will be forced to take matters into our own hands and, in the tradition of Martin Luther King and Gandhi, take unlawful actions against an unjust government." He clicks off.

"Are you crazy?" asks Mommy, now afraid. In between "He's losing it" and "Are you crazy?" lies a whole sea of meaning.

"I'm mailing it to Hamburger tomorrow," he says. "If she doesn't respond before Wednesday, we're taking the street."

"Our own street?"

Daddy looks around for a padded envelope, and sees instead a potential ally, the girl who just aced her test on India.

"Hey, punko," he says. "Want to show Longview what we're made of?"

I think of the post-me albums, the diapers, the boys who make diaper jokes about Gandhi.

"Do you want me to get hit by a car on purpose?"

"No, just clean up your room before the meeting tomorrow."

"They're not going to go in my room."

MY BED'S BEEN MADE. I trot downstairs, sling around the banister at the base. I pile some hot artichoke on a saltine. The chairs are out, evenly staggered, Mommy style. She's very exacting about the chairs.

"Good job, Mom."

Mom? It just comes out, her new name. Is this how it happens? One day you're "Mommy, change me, feed me, sprinkle talc all over my naked body," the next day you're complimenting her on folding-chair spacing. Mommy doesn't notice.

"I need to review the talking points," she says. "Don't eat all the dip before people get here."

People get here. The gardener lady's wearing lipstick, maybe hoping to meet another enraged single. She's dreaming, though, because except for me and the widower, it's all furious couples in sweaters.

Daddy has maps, crudités, an easel.

"That was my easel," I say, to nobody. Nobody asked to borrow it, either.

"The morning commute won't be affected by the one-way chokehold Longview is imposing, since cars can still use both Longview and Hillview to go west," he says, drawing parallel sedans going west. "But we want to get some folks out to protest Longview in the mornings, too. Bruce? Lillian?

"The evenings are when we have our real battle. As the streets parallel, we will get all of Longview's eastbound commuter traffic." He draws a fat line of trucks trying to go east.

"Not on our watch!" screams a Bruce.

"Not our kids," says a wife, pointing at me. There's applause. I represent something, a kid who might run into the street, basted by a car that should have been on Longview.

"She knows not to run into the street," says Daddy. "But, as I said in the tape I sent City Hall, some kids don't. And that's why we're not going to let these Longviewers commute in peace, day or night, until we get this one-way farce reversed and traffic is flowing freely on both streets in both directions again!" He draws cars going in both directions.

"Sign up for a morning or evening shift depending on your work schedule. Stay-at-home moms, we need you right now."

Mommy calls them non-working mothers.

"I WISH my parents cared about something," says Kira. She's using ketchup packets to make a rag look bloody for a skit we have to do about *The Pearl*. She's going to play the mother and me the father. A doll is playing our baby. A Tic Tac is playing the pearl.

"You live on a cul-de-sac," I say. "What's the problem?"

"My dad has no interest in community service."

I don't mind playing the father. I've borrowed one of Daddy's old jackets, and I'm roughing it up with a stapler. I'm going to need a mustache. Luckily, I have no breasts. Kira's costume is from our linen closet. Her hair's in braids.

"The kids who got *Of Mice and Men* are really lucky," she says, trying to make our doll look deader. "I'd kill for that one."

.　.　.

BOTH PHONE LINES are busy over the weekend. One of the Bruces is getting divorced. He'll be departing our street for a condo, a support group.

"I'm losing a real soldier," says Daddy.

There was the time this Bruce stayed up half the night coming up with the perfect clip art for the "Hillview Is Not a Highway" flyer, the time he called Mayor May a cunt. After a while Daddy just says, "A soldier," and Mommy and I fill in the rest of his sad.

Over on Line 2, Kira sheds her uterine lining for the first time. My bridge almost collapses with the news. My uterine lining remains intact. Happily married Bruce calls on Line 1 to talk to Daddy, now his one remaining Bruce, suddenly the only Bruce he can count on.

The town, for some reason, is not moved by the tape.

"Do you know what this means?" Daddy laughs, maybe thrilled to be ignored. "Hamburger wants war. Are you ready to mobilize?"

We're sitting around the kitchen table Tuesday evening. Mommy's drowning a tea biscuit in decaf. I'm coloring in my maison for French. I draw mon téléphone in ma chambre.

"La Ligne Deux," I write.

"I'll call Bruce," he says.

"I don't know," says Mommy.

"I have a Pakistan ditto," I say. "But then I can help."

Help means collating the new flyers, practicing our chants. The new flyers say "One Way? No Way!"

"I have to be at work early tomorrow," says Mommy later. She's in her nightgown, under her lamp. He's pacing the den, pretending to yell at cars. "So keep an eye on him on Longview," she says. "Don't let him do anything crazy."

"If he tries to do something crazy, how will I stop him?"

"Just tell him to stop."

WEDNESDAY, A.M., Daddy and I are standing in the shoulder of the other street, minivan gusts whipping our "One Way? No Way!" signs back into our chests. Daddy's scanning for his friends. Never-married gardener is a no-show. Happily married Bruce not present.

The cars just go west. There's not much to see.

The widower friend shows up wearing his flannel jacket, dusted with dog hair. He and Daddy sort of grip each other hello, and then he leaves. We wait. A couple of women in terry-cloth walk by, but we're not sure if they're Longviewers or Hill-viewers or just power walkers.

"Maybe tomorrow I'll bring Kira, so we have more people."

"The whole street's in denial," says Daddy. "People completely disregarded the sign-up sheet. The stay-at-home moms stayed at home. But wait until they see how much traffic our street eats tonight. We'll stand in front of our house with signs. I'll make extra copies at work, so everyone has one to hold."

LE MATIN PROCHAIN, LE MÊME. Except Daddy makes me and Kira sing a song. It has to do with sticking to a union till the day we die. We sang it last night on the sidewalk in front of our house. Daddy passed out lyrics. Mommy and I didn't need them. The union song is from a cassette Daddy keeps in the car for long car trips. We have other tapes, but Daddy never plays them. What he does play now are cassettes from Line 1's answering machine—Sorry, Alan, work's been crazy, tae kwon do, Karen caught the flu. Mommy urges Daddy to delete, but he's starting a list by the phone.

"Not flu season yet!" it says.

FRIDAY MORNING, I lie in bed for a few minutes after I wake up, sliding the lump under my left nipple. It seems wider than usual, wider than the right. I scramble to my desk, flip through the index of *Exploring Life Science* until I find Puberty, female.

"Breast bud and papilla swell and a small mound is present; areola diameter is enlarged."

This is it, this is Puberty, female.

AT ASSEMBLY, Kira tells me she can't come anymore. Assembly's in the gym. It's Croatia Day. Puffed-sleeved maidens wave handkerchiefs while the teachers shush us. Every last Friday of the month, we're herded into the bleachers to disrespect dancers from politically unstable lands.

"It's only been two days," I say. "We haven't even done civil disobedience yet."

"Why do you keep touching your breast?"

"I'm not. Why can't you? Is your mom scared?"

"No. Your dad's—"

The dancers' clogs make a sudden racket on the shellacked floor.

"What? My dad's what?"

"Your dad's awesome. But I don't live in that neighborhood."

· · ·

MONDAY MORNING, we stand on a lawn on Longview instead. Even the widower's given up, gone back to his usual routine, transferring photographs of his late wife out of albums that have lost their stick. Our signs have wrinkled, curled. They're already mementos of this time.

"Longview is kind of scary without sidewalks, Daddy."

"They could build sidewalks," snaps Daddy. "There's certainly enough room on their lawns. Then they'd have sidewalks."

"Where's the lady who gardens?" I say.

"Who?" he says.

"Bruce never comes."

"He's redoing his dining room."

"What's wrong with his dining room?"

"Gene Flusser!"

The driver of a passing car is a famous Longviewer, the one in bed with May Hamburger. Daddy drops his sign and gives Flusser's bumper the finger.

"Is the finger in the tradition of Martin Luther King?" I ask.

"This one is," he says. He leaves the finger up, for everybody. I put mine up, aiming it at the other street and also a little at him.

I guess we're showing Longview what we're made of.

We're made of cells. We're made of fatty tissues, which we either fear or desire, depending on where they deposit. We get labeled in textbooks—organ, organelle. We give traffic the finger.

Except traffic must have seen the finger, because Gene Flusser's walking back, from kind of far. He can't drive back because the street's one way.

"Daddy, stop," I say.

"Stop what?" he says, tucking his middle finger back into his fist.

"He's coming."

"I see him—Gene!"

"Alan! Aren't you cold standing here?" asks Flusser.

"We're staying warm," says Daddy.

"Who's this young lady?"

"She's a fighter."

It's all very friendly, Longview, Hillview. What the view is of, nobody can say.

"Shouldn't you be in school?" says Flusser, extending a handshake to me.

"I have a note." One of my hands rests on my jacket where the new breast should be. The other shoots out to shake. "But I'm learning a lot out here. You guys could use some sidewalks. Why'd you get out of the car, Mr. Flusser?"

"I forgot my lunch, so I'm going back to get it."

He doesn't even look at our signs.

I'M ON YEARBOOK NOW. I write poems about assemblies, come up with captions for boys who ignore me.

Kira and I didn't stop being friends because of the street. We're still friends. Now we're crying about the Joads. Now we're sanding boats. They will float on half an inch of water in a stoppered sink. They will never know the sea.

Mommy has a new enemy: the phone company.

"Thieves," she says, highlighting my calls on the bill. But her heart's not in the hate. The folding chairs stay folded in the basement. My easel stays folded.

Daddy's not doing mornings on Longview anymore. He

decided it was best to conserve our energy for our own street, because people in gridlock are more likely to be sympathetic. He's not doing evenings on our street anymore either, though, except that he sits in gridlock with the others on his way home from work.

But walking home, sometimes I think I see him, one block away, planted on our sidewalk, a man with salt and pepper ringing his bald spot, a man with a Windbreaker, Longview's worst nightmare, the only man with enough love to turn the tide the other way.

http://www.msjiz/boxx374/mpeg

SHE WAS A GRIEVING CHAMP—black bra, black jeans, two competing bereavement groups. She kept my father's computing magazines by his side of the bed, in case he came back to life and needed to order some outdated PCs. She kept his diabetic candies on top of the computing magazines, in case he came back still diabetic. When I came to visit, we looked at pictures in her bed and sucked his candies. I lay in his spot. She slept in his shirts. He had T-shirts championing places he'd vacationed, runs to cure diseases that hadn't killed him.

She framed photos of him we'd ignored for years—him by the waterfall with the fanny pack, him driving cross-country shirtless before any of us knew him, before men in this country wore fanny packs. My mother made copies for me to take back to Brooklyn. I put the copies in a box under my desk, a box that held knitting needles, a pane of lighthouse stamps from the week I thought I would collect stamps, free NYC condoms. The condom wrappers had the subway map on them, in case you needed to know how to get somewhere while erect.

I left the city every few weeks to be unemployed at my mother's house and pretend I was there to fix her computer. First we made dinner. I strained broccoli while she tried to convince me that I would like working with people. She folded napkins and I told her to join a book club. Dessert was always called "a treat."

Then we did albums. The baby ones were best, before the house, the sprinkler, the unlisted number. But pictures at the house were still better than pictures somewhere else, any vacation museum-weary in retrospect. Why had we chosen Quebec that year? Why had we been to tombs, to caves, rushed into darkness by locals to learn millennia along the wall? Stalactites and stalagmites, limestone blown out by flash, cousins waving glow sticks at roller rinks, my father not even in them because he was taking them, leading our family out onto jetties, teaching me that buoy wasn't the same as boy. I thought their white Styrofoam heads bobbing were a new kind of boy.

"I need an empty dishwasher before bed," said my mother. "But I hate to bend."

"I'll bend."

I put the forks where I remembered. I stacked damp Tupperware where it didn't belong. I glided from room to room in my mother's house, into the laundry room to see what was new there, down to the garage with dinner's garbage. I peed an unnecessary number of times. There's nothing to do here but pee, I thought. I needed the internet. This was before you brought your own computer to your mother's house, before the internet was in every room, so I went to the room designated for hers. Lots of warnings popped up during the dial-up song—my mother needed a new computer—but I had no idea how to fix that. I went to a website for idealists looking for jobs. None of them were ideal. I started opening old WordPerfect files, mostly letters my father had written—angry letters asking the cave tour company for a refund, boring letters to me at camp.

"It's too bad you don't love your swim instructor. Diving can be tough. I am enclosing your June report card. What happened in Home and Careers? Regardless, the rest of it is a knockout. Way to go!"

I was still no good at home or careers. Grades predicted something, maybe that you'd only be good at getting good grades. I missed quarterly reminders of what adults expected of me. I missed the old Courier font, 1994 in the corner. His letters were written years before he had gotten sick and had no trace of sick in them—no battle metaphors or gastrointestinal reports.

"The fight goes on. Today was a good day. I even managed to get some ice cream down."

He wrote daily when he was too sick to work anymore, bleak cheerful missives, cc'd to too many people. I wanted to check to see if he'd written a final letter to me only, something he hadn't had time to print out. I wanted last words, a story I'd never heard about summers at Lake Luzerne, a drugged-out road trip with an old girlfriend, paternal wisdom that might move me to tears. *The meaning of life is love. It's never too late to learn how to dive.* I scrolled down the Recent Documents section—different versions of my résumé, a bill from the urn people, and a link, http://www.msjiz/boxx374/mpeg. The link took me to a thirty-second video of two topless women boxing, punching each other and grunting. The women's breasts swung dangerously. They sneered at each other, but it was a joke, it wasn't real. The blonde pushed the brunette against the ropes, and the brunette snapped back. She raised her fists and the video froze.

I closed the window, then shut down the whole machine. Of course, all men looked at porn. He must have found the boxing late one night when he couldn't sleep, searching, not exactly knowing what he was looking for. I breathed out through my nose. My own darkness reached toward my father's darkness, both of us nosy in our sleeplessness, both of us with oily noses.

Still, the sick are supposed to be holy, empty of desire. Their flesh is pallid and their eyes are bright. They tend to be hairless. Maybe he wanted to have desire again, maybe he got bored waiting to die. Well, what was he supposed to be looking at? Girls of the Herman D. Weiss Center for Radiology and Oncology? Bald Sluts? Barely Breathing?

I hurried to my old room, lay down in my old bed, and then sat back up to admire the glow-in-the-dark stars I had pasted on the closet door, because my parents hadn't let me put them on the ceiling.

MY MOTHER was having breakfast the next morning when she saw me come down the steps.

"Six a.m.! How nice of you to join me."

I'd snuck up on her being happy. She was furious most of the time, but here she was, allowing herself a moment of peace in a blouse, spooning cereal while it was still dark outside.

"Do you want some? I made tapioca."

"Mommy," I said. "You seem good today."

"Yeah." She twisted her mouth. "I'm wonderful."

She drove away to have a wonderful day at work. I did a search for "water filters" because I wanted to protect her from the carcinogens of northern New Jersey. When I typed the "w," "women boxing" appeared as a previous search. He had sought them out. The boxers had enormous breasts. My mother's breasts were tiny, a few inches of raised skin, nipples the size of pennies. Did he dream of swinging breasts, of humiliation, knockouts, defeat? I thought about my own breasts. They would leak milk one day, harden with lumps the next. Blood would be mopped off the floor. I sat there for so long that the computer switched over to its screen saver, spiraling into infinity.

In my mother's house, back when it was my parents' house, back when it was just my house—when I was an adolescent who went to high school and had long hair and lived in a house—my father and I would sometimes bump into each other in the middle of the night. He would go down to the kitchen to sneak cookies, and I'd go to the bathroom to inspect my pimples. Some were red, puffed-up, painful, others purple and faded, and I diligently spread prescription acne cream onto each one. The cream did nothing, but the smell palliated me.

"Dad, when did your acne go away?"

"Mine was worse than yours. I was a pizza face."

"Are those cookies sugar-free? Sometimes I want to rip my face off."

"Please don't."

"When I was little I wanted pimples and braces. I *wanted* them."

WHEN I TYPED the letter "r" into the search engine in my mother's computer, the first thing that came up was "radiation enteritis," a condition in which the lining of the small intestine gets eroded by radiation therapy. The patient has diarrhea about once every half hour, and winds up having to be fed through hyper-alimentation—a bag pumps liquid nutrients into a vein. The patient takes to wearing a forest-green backpack with the bag in it. The patient and my mother begin to affectionately refer to the bag as "hyper-al," like it's a buddy, it's Hyper Al! Me and Al, we're going on a little day hike through the house here to, ya know, calm Al down. My mother says things like "Thank God for hyper-al." But then my father needs a different bag, a bag to hold what comes out of him, a clear bag so you can see greenish orange liquid sloshing around in it, and this bag he doesn't bother to hide, because, what the fuck, guess what? He's dying. I load the dishwasher and won't admit it. Then he makes a joke. Then he's dead.

What was his joke? No, it wasn't dirty. It was about me.

"Thanks for loading the dishwasher," he said. "I never thought I'd live to see the day."

MY FATHER was dead and my mother was loading the dishwasher in his "Guatemala: Heart of the Mayan World" T-shirt. She stuffed some forks into a tough spot. She rinsed empty olive containers, readying them for their new life as leftover storage vessels. Widowhood seemed to be about managing containers, telling you there was no longer coleslaw in what had been labeled "Coleslaw." Or maybe that was adulthood. I wasn't sure which hood she represented anymore. I didn't know what I was standing against.

"You need a water filter," I told my mother.

"You need a job," she said. She ran unfiltered tap water over her hands, then shook them into the sink.

"I thought you wanted me to work with people," I said.

"I'm not people. Dry this."

"I'm going to show you the latest filtration technology," I said. "Carbon. Charcoal."

We dried for a while. She thought I could look into a career in environmental regulation. I thought I didn't care about the environment, just her house. She was doing her part, reusing containers, repurposing her husband's shirts. Plastic bags metastasized under the sink, and there was still a lawn to poison and mow, but she could replace my father's car with a hybrid, or not replace it at all. She had her own car. She could be a one-car family.

"Ma, what do you think about recycling Daddy's computing magazines?"

"He loved the computer," she said.

"*PC Today* from March 1997? He wouldn't buy a PC from March 1997 if he were here today."

She paused drying. She liked to think about what he would do if he were here. I had convinced her to do a number of things by invoking his hypothetical opinion.

"He'd want you to get a haircut. He'd think the ends were getting scraggly."

"He'd definitely replace the microwave if it was melting."

"He wouldn't want me to have a job answering phones."

That last one was a lie. If he were here, I'd be answering phones somewhere, a receptionist without grief, assistant to a man who didn't remind me of my father, because men that age wouldn't.

THE WATER FILTER SEARCH was on. I seated my mother in her computer chair. I wanted to foster technological confidence. Do an internet search for your mother, and she'll get a list of results. Teach your mother to search, and she'll search for a lifetime.

My mother stared at her computer screen like it was the control panel in the White House Situation Room, while I explained how to move a mouse.

"Down, Ma! Not up! Scroll down.

"The blinking cursor," I said. "That's you.

"Type 'w,'" I said.

Men Against Violence

MY FRIEND is marrying a man against violence. He founded a club called "Men Against Violence" in college, when he was not yet sleeping with my friend.

"It's not that impressive to be against violence," I said, "if you would never be violent anyway."

My friend was impressed. She promoted him to boyfriend and they moved to Washington, D.C., to lobby for the religion that celebrates the holidays of all other religions. I promised to take the train, the bus, but never settled on a mode of transportation. It's hard to get to Washington when you don't want to go there.

Soon they were back—law school, divinity school, nothing violent. My friend carried the Bible with her everywhere. She used it to hold our table at lunch because nobody would steal the Bible. I got falafel on the Bible. She paid for lunch. My friend promised to keep me posted, to send more photographs of them getting engaged.

WHEN MY FRIEND'S FIANCÉ founded "Men Against Violence," a lesbian at our college didn't like it. A room full of men talking. What were they talking about? There was no way for us to know. I said they talked about porn. I said they were scared about violence in porn. This was college, when we were all more scared about violence in porn. But porn won.

The lesbian attended the men's meeting and screamed at them. She was the kind of lesbian who could shame a room full of men into disbanding their club according to the same principles upon which it was founded. Then the lesbian dated another friend of mine, a bisexual, and was violent toward her. It shed new light on the lesbian's fury. After college, my bisexual friend dated men again, only men, men who wouldn't hurt anyone, men who would have been against violence if they had gone to our college. Nobody was good-looking. Maybe being bad-looking made them want to be violent, and that's why they had formed a club not to be. This explanation still made sense when I attended the wedding of my friend and the man who had founded "Men Against Violence."

AT THE WEDDING, I made a toast. It was a job assigned to me because I was "good with words." I wondered if I would have to let my friend minister my wedding because she was good with God. My toast was not very good. I did not mention the club my friend's new husband had formed and disbanded in college, though the club was all I wanted to say about him. I said my friend was marrying someone with a cool beard.

I had seen cooler beards. I had seen cooler beards at this wedding, but most of the men with beards had girlfriends, assigned to sit next to them in case the water glasses got mixed up.

When had my friend made so many new friends? Were they all ministers? I met Methodists, Episcopalians, Unitarians. The girls were pretty and seemed concerned about race relations. The men were quieter, chewing behind their beards, like they had always been heading in the direction of wearing a tie at this table. Couples danced whether or not they were going to make it through the year. They were going to make it through the night, was the message, so back off. They didn't know that I had backed off years ago, when all this was still for the taking.

"Dr. King espoused nonviolent resistance," said a Presbyterian in a tube dress.

"He wouldn't have been violent anyway," I sort of whispered.

The bride and groom sat by themselves at a two-person desk, which I later learned was called the "Sweethearts' Table." They were in charge of what we valued tonight—ethical shrimp, token gay ministers, gift packets of seeds, nonviolent porn. They thanked the wedding guests for taking planes from all over the world to form this community. They handed a mic back and forth, and seemed moved.

Somehow, the two of them moved back to the town where we had gone to college. They must have liked it there. My friend became a minister to the students at the college, but it's not called a minister when it's students. It's called a chaplain. Violence might mean something other than violence, too, at this college. I always thought violence meant a punch in the face, a knife to the throat, but the students at this college meant whenever you felt violated. That could be anytime.

RIGHT NOW I am violating my friend and her husband by telling their story. I am violating the college and all its clubs. Someone could point out that a girl at the college was once a victim of actual murder. There is a tree with her name at the base, on a plaque. The tree blocks the view from a hill where we used to sit. The tree violates the view. I didn't know the girl, or miss her, because she went to the college after we went, after my friend's husband's club was formed and disbanded, but before my friend and her husband moved back. I didn't know the guy who killed her, but I know violence has to mean what it says, and it shuts everybody up when it says it.

Welcome Lilah

ON THE BUS, I was jealous. I was jealous of the girl in front of me, jealous of the girl diagonal. I was jealous of the elderly Chinese woman sleeping by the window. It was the Chinatown Bus. The bus was taking me to see a guy who had come to see me twice, a guy who held doors, a guy who told me I was cute like he was trying to ward something off. He would find all of these girls cute. Any of us could step off the bus and be his girlfriend.

By the time I got off the bus, I was done with him. He was there anyway, waiting to take my bag. The problem was that it was his birthday. I had a box of Italian cookies and a card I had written on the bus.

"You are special," I had written. It was the only thing I could think of that wasn't a lie. Everyone was special. "I hope you like cookies . . . ," I had added. That was a lie. I knew he liked cookies. The cookies were in one of those white boxes that make baked goods seem promising.

"Some may have broken," I said. "They'll still be good."

"I can't wait," he said. He really liked cookies. He had told me many times, but what else did I know about him? He cared about real estate. His mother was dead. So was my dad. Cookies and real estate. I did not care. This was my first boyfriend since the last one.

Does it matter that we were in Boston? We had to stay at his dad's house in Newton, since my unwanted boyfriend wouldn't rent an apartment. He only wanted to own. I wanted to meet the dad, but we got in too late. We put the white box on the white countertop, an island bisecting the kitchen, just like in my mother's house. His dad had the same cheeses in the refrigerator, the same jams. The house had the same quiet.

"Welcome Lilah!"

On a bright square of printer paper, the dad had left me a note, a note that maybe needed a comma.

"I made a reservation for tomorrow," said the son.

"For all of us?" He'd mentioned father, sister, maybe grandpa.

"No, just us."

I didn't know his father, his sister, or his grandpa, but there had been a chance they'd be people I'd like to know. I wanted to watch him with people he didn't find cute. Maybe I could blend into those people. Though maybe he found his sister cute—not unfeasible.

"I'm going to have one." He opened the white box, and held up the kind with a fruit center, the dark womb of cookie.

"I wanted to meet your sister."

"You will."

I wouldn't. After the birthday ended, I was getting on a bus going the other way. Still, I liked the idea of the sister. She was a singer, a guitar cradler. She wrote funny songs about tingly soap. She had a nickname. She was a lesbian. They made up songs together and missed their mom together and posed together on their dad's refrigerator.

My name was hard to nick. Lie, I guess. Or Ah. This is my girlfriend, Ah. She's sighing with pleasure. She's having an orgasm. That's not a problem for Ah. That's not our problem. Our problem is death. The night her father died, Ah tore the dad and husband cartoons off the refrigerator, because she didn't want to make fun of a family member who was no longer in the family. She tore down the couples in bed, hating each other. They didn't look like her parents anyway.

"No, Bean, dinner's going to be just the two of us," he said on the landline with his sister, slinking cordless past his own fridge cartoons. He tiptoed to get something from the pantry, and I watched his pants, dark gray with a little stretch in them. He shook a box of cereal. I saw that he wasn't a boy, my boyfriend, but a small, clean man. He had come straight from work. Work was law. Real estate was his area. He had a client dying of AIDS who was suing his sister over a house they'd both inherited. I liked him best when he talked about the case.

WE WOKE UP LATE on the birthday, Saturday. The father was already gone. We walked around a pond. He took me to the Newton library and read me a poem in one of those soundproof study rooms. I didn't really hear the poem. When we left the library, I tried to call my friends who'd had a party the month before, the party where we'd met, but both of their voicemails picked up after no rings.

"Hey," I said, over dinner with just us, "when you turned twenty, did you care about real estate then?"

We were high up on plump cushions, intimidated by our steaks.

"I guess. Sure." He started to cut a piece.

"How about when you were sixteen?" I looked at my knife, fork, perfect on the white cloth. I didn't want to bloody them. It occurred to me that he would pay for dinner and that the paying would matter after I broke up with him. I was taking pains to wait until the birthday was over, but unless I waited a week, it would still be his birthday. And he would have paid even if I had broken up over dinner, to show that he would.

"No, then I wanted to make films, I guess—documentaries."

"What did you want to document?"

"I wasn't thinking about what I would shoot. My mother."

He excused himself to the bathroom, and I told the waiter it was his birthday. The waiter frowned like he knew I didn't want to be the one surreptitiously ordering the one-candled mousse. It wasn't my fault dinner had been changed to just us. If I didn't sing the song, who would? It was his birthday.

Every time this guy went to the deli, he embarrassed me with deli flowers. He got cookies for himself. He apologized. He was officially good, and I enjoyed berating myself for not appreciating his goodness. What pleasure I took in scooting ahead to a door before he had a chance to hold it. I'd shove myself through, sometimes grabbing it back and holding it for him, winning a race against chivalry nobody but me knew I had signed up for.

When we got back to the house, it was just like the night before, except for feeling full in an expensive way. The dad was asleep again. The lights were left on in the kitchen again. We started making tea. We started making out. I got down on my knees. I was happier than I'd been, suddenly. It was like when a kid goes underwater and gets to hear her own quiet for the first time all day. Down there was sealed off from his mild wrong, the vague suck of him. I sucked. I held on. The teapot squealed and I hissed, "Turn it off."

"Maybe we should go up?"

Then we were jogging through the living room, past candelabra in the fireplace, and Marilyn Monroe framed in the corner, and I'm thinking, "The dad decorates?" I wished we'd stayed in the kitchen. But he had his pants. He was up the stairs. The sheets on the guest bed hadn't been changed recently, since there had been no guests. The room had permanent guest bed smell. The room was maybe a room for a visitor who'd come to see the sick parent, a room for a visiting female relative who always knows more than you do about the statistics of your parent's illness, the chances of her sibling's or her cousin's survival, and so unpacks her toiletries and waits at the kitchen table to ambush you with printer pages, with sighs, when you're trying to just get home from school, to snack on fruit-filled cookies or jams or whatever it is you snack on, while your parent is fighting statistics upstairs.

Ovarian—does anyone survive that? What my dad had, nobody survives. Okay, somebody does, and the guy gets an article written about him in a journal of hope. One guy, hang gliding, balding in a wet suit, gets to continue to do extreme sports. My dad had sports, but maybe they weren't extreme enough. Nobody wants to rescue a guy who gets to continue jogging.

My bag was on the floor, clothes erupting out of it, starting their sickening sprawl across the carpet, underwear hang gliding in the jeans. I was at the door, pushing in the lock, but it wouldn't catch.

"Lilah, he's definitely sleeping."

"Maybe we should go back downstairs."

Documentarian—that's what everyone wants to be before they decide to be something else. It's a good imagined profession. Creative, yet factual. Lions, yet poor people. Shots through the grass, the hut, the chew. Or snakes that don't chew, that just suck the bump down.

"I have to go to the bathroom," I said. I went down the hall and peed, peed through the turn-on swell, then washed my hands with a gray ball of soap. It didn't tingle. I had never had a boyfriend I hadn't liked. The one before this, I had liked him a lot. He was captain of his street hockey team. He carried his stick around, even on days when there was no practice, even though he was thirty-three. He probably still carries it around.

Back in the guest room, I said, "Listen." I said, "I feel." He backed onto the guest bed, pulled me on top of him to stop "I feel."

"Okay," I said. He smiled, relieved. We were still on. It was still his birthday. The track lighting lit the wine scabbed on his lip, gave his mouth a little Marilyn in the corner. I sat on his mouth. That had happened every time since we'd met, and made it feel like we'd known each other longer.

"Keep going," I said. It was my version of "Don't stop."

"Good!" I said.

"You're doing great," I said.

"Can you breathe?" I said.

He hummed the first few bars of "Happy birthday."

"Hold it," I said, climbing off his head. "You were doing great stuff, but I feel a little nauseous right now."

"From the wine?"

"A little. I'm not going to throw up."

Disappointed, he tried to make it up with a snuggle, a hair-stroke/whisper move. I felt sorry for myself for all the times I had been on the other side, whispering. It wasn't just the

hockey captain. There were others, guys who'd let me hope-
lessly cuddle them for months, years. How had they let me go
on, me not knowing what they knew? In return, I would agree
to let them be depressed.

Nobody had ever liked anybody.

My Allergies Will Charm You

HE HAD FOUND ME on the internet, and now I was going back to the internet. He could know me through my college newspaper quotes ("The new student center is a costly mistake"), my discussion board tips for fermenting your own sauerkraut, the time I disagreed with an actress's choice of shoe. He could check the friend sites to see if I had any new friends, if I was growing my hair.

I am growing it. It's getting less blond every day. I wasn't blond for very long. Long enough to make some mistakes. The dating sites are full of them. Pics of them at sunset somewhere. Their favorite books that meant something to them. Them just wanting someone to make them laugh, stay up all night laughing.

Some like blondes or brunettes, but the terms are dated now.

They want nerds who like to be tied up, tits in a certain shape. Are my tits shaped like the tits of request? I wonder.

He had found me, searching girls with my zip code, body type, religious beliefs. I see these girls, knocking down toilet paper at the same bodegas, reaching for lettuce from the same salad bars, one-hundred-twenty-pounders who never think about God.

He had found me at work, in between trips to the copy machine, where he was Xeroxing his résumé for a different job, one he wouldn't need to call a day job, even if it took place during the day. He had found me, or a thumb-sized version of me, sunburned at a street fair, jubilant in a tube top.

"Nice funnel cake," he wrote.

"Thank you!"

I volleyed back his better jokes, introduced new queries. We sent additional pics—me squeezing my tits together, him toasting the end of the calendar year. We exchanged birth towns, sibling counts. We mentioned coffee, but decided on drinks. Coffee always gets mentioned. Drinks always wins.

I arrived, not tube-topped or jubilant, but cardiganned, dehydrated, on time. I slurped an icy gin. I retold my best stories without remembering why they were important. In "Every Foreign Country I Visit Reminds Me of Long Island," I forgot to say that's where I was from. In "The Summer I Spent Working with Pigeons," I left out what we were trying to understand about the cognition of those birds. In "I Ate a Pot Cookie and Believed Myself to Be Already Dead," I omitted the emergency room I had taken myself to, where I had asked the other dead people how long they'd been waiting.

"About an hour."

"Wow."

My date told me he'd once played a sexually abused kid in a movie. They had told him to look sad but hadn't explained why. Later, he'd rented it. I felt sorry for him, as if he'd really been abused. I unbuttoned my cardigan. What was the plan—to heal fictional sexual abuse with the promise of actual sexual consent? I detoured into "My Allergies Will Charm You," and finished up with "Jesus Was the First Guy with a Jesus Complex," a surprising favorite. We compared hand sizes. Our hands were different sizes. Soon we were negotiating—maybe we should go somewhere, and where should we go? Somewhere.

My date and I didn't start dating that night. We went to bed instead. Bed was fine, bed was bed, except the time he held his hand over my mouth. That was pretty good. I think it was an accident, though, because I never saw that hand again.

"Xerox that," I should have said. Make me twenty copies. I'll tell the pigeon story with all the good parts, with the Skinner boxes, and the pellets, and the time I caught a bird that escaped using just a flashlight and my hand.

Keep an Eye on It

THEY SAID keep an eye on it, they said it was nothing, they took its picture, they took a sample, they burned it, they froze it, they biopsied it, they told me to come back in a year, they winced when they saw me coming, they wrote down everything I said or dictated it to a woman who had to be in the room for legal reasons, they wrote me a prescription, they said, "You write fiction, that must be interesting."

In fiction, it's never benign.

The Lucky Lady

HE WASN'T LOOKING AT ME. He didn't know me. I told him I'd had sex in his room once.

"Not with me," he said.

"A different guy lived here," I said. "Before you. He collected banjos. The bed was over there. So were the banjos."

I squeaked open a drawer that was already a little open. It was filled with closed bottles of pills.

"There is a lot of medication in that drawer," I said.

"I have cancer," he said. "I have a girlfriend."

"What kind?"

"The pretty kind. Read my blog," he said. Over there it said he had cancer, too. It was Halloween. Everyone was smoking his cancer pot and wearing bracelets to support his cancer's cure. I was sitting on his bed, reading his blog, unfortunately dressed as a pirate. His cancer hadn't had bracelets or blogs before he had it. It didn't have cosmetics-sponsored walks. It was in need of a celebrity.

I went to see if the girlfriend was my kind of pretty. Her face didn't answer the question. She was one of many sporks. Everyone thought they were forks. New sporks kept arriving, hugging each other, whooping. There was a guy dressed as a drive-in movie theater—miniature cars in a miniature parking lot, a projector that beamed a short film onto his chest.

"His birthday's Halloween," people said, as though that explained why he had to do this.

There was a bedbug and a bed. There were blinged-out rev-olutionaries, zombies and robots, apocalyptic survival strate-gies for men who wouldn't survive a subway delay. Where were the other pirates? Nobody was even scary.

I couldn't figure out the cancer guy's costume. Cancer patient? Flatware? He was wearing gray pajamas. He was now on the bed we'd never had sex on, or, as he probably thought of it, his bed. He took a hit to cool his nausea.

"Captain Hook," he said, though I had no hook.

"I just started reading 'Immuno Suppress This, Bitch,'" I told him. I held up the glow-lit device that made it possible to read his blog at his party.

"Take a bracelet, Captain," he said. "Become a fan of me."

He passed the pipe. I soothed future tumors with it.

YOU COULD become fans of the bloggers now, follow them, stream their blogs right into your glow-lit device, blogs about the obsolescence of blogs. Still, I appreciated the form. The guy who debated with himself about whether poor kids should be taught in a semicircle on a rug—the way he'd been taught— or the way where the kids are assigned to homerooms named after the universities he'd gone to. The guy who was trying to get you to compost your dead relatives instead of embalming them. The guy doing Gay Doctors in War Zones with his gay doctor boyfriend. I'd dated the boyfriend briefly, back when he was still bisexual. I'd dated all of them, or wanted to. The blogs were what I had left or what I would never have. I followed.

My cancer patient was blogging every day like it was his last. He dunked himself in icy waterfalls to ring in the New Year. He waded out into the middle of freezing lakes in trunks that showed off his tattoos, his scars. He went whitewater rafting with amputees. He proposed to his girlfriend in song. Everything was recorded, linked to, tweeted, re-tweeted.

But at night, he still had cancer. Steroids kept him awake and chatting with empathetic women. He was cancer-nice to us, or what I later found out was us. The girlfriend was a saint, was his rock, was asleep. I was awake. Julie was awake. We commented on his posts with "Hooray"s for remission, "Oh nooooo!"s for new tumors, "That sucks" for side effects, and he zoomed back and forth between us, frantically emoticonning his approval of our jokes, comforting us when we were rejected by healthy men.

"I'll kill him," he wrote. "What do I have to lose?"

"Ha ha," I wrote. "Ha ha."

I didn't know what he had to lose. He didn't have any money. He was throwing a fund-raiser for his upcoming treatment, and you could buy bracelets off the site, mugs, hoodies. People biked, walked, ran, and sometimes swam in his honor, to send him parasailing with other terminal cases who wanted to challenge death in a non-hospital venue, and he in turn featured them as "Supporters," "Besties," or "Awesome Ambassadors of Jamie." He was his own cause. I liked causes. I was the kind to get particularly attached to a political prisoner, the kind who stood in front of embassies with decade-old pictures of the prisoner, the kind who handed out bullet-pointed info sheets to people just shopping near the embassy. I would go to Jamie's fund-raiser. I would raise funds.

The problem was that I wasn't good at asking people for money. I had been a terrible Girl Scout, dawdling around the neighborhood without a uniform, underselling the Thin Mints. My parents wouldn't buy me the uniform. Without it, a Girl Scout is just a girl. I drafted an email with a link to Jamie's newest video, an infomercial starring him warning teens to get checked early and often for what he wished he didn't have.

"He really has cancer!!!" flashed under his face, in case the vicious internet thought he looked too cute for the disease.

I cc'd former bosses, people's parents, my own two aunts. I mentioned bands that might play the fund-raiser—local bands to fight his non-localized cancer. I sent Jamie twenty dollars. But I couldn't send the email. I didn't want him to be another cause people deleted, another petition to not sign.

Maybe I could just tell my friends to buy the merch. The girlfriend designed the merch. The hoodie was cute—it had a silkscreened PET scan of Jamie's most recent tumor, with a universal No symbol slashed through it. You could toast Jamie's survival with "Immuno Suppress This, Bitch" shot glasses. There would be karaoke at the fund-raiser, and the couple was already taking duet requests via e-Jukebox. Each song cost a dollar. My fund-raising skills didn't really seem needed.

"What can I do?" I asked him. I pictured myself grocery shopping after his next surgery, making pharmacy runs to several different pharmacies until I found the anti-inflammatory he needed to counteract whatever gene therapy had inflamed. He didn't get bald from this therapy, and he looked pretty good, though sometimes lymph leaked out of his groin.

"Just be you," he wrote.

Being me didn't pay for cancer treatment. The newest trials had promise, but there weren't enough survivors of Jamie's cancer for a walk celebrating those who'd survived. Walks were for the lucky cancers, the lipstick cancers, though even within those cancers, the unlucky could be shunned, kicked off a survivors' board if the disease recurred or they died. I'd heard of this happening in my Long Island town. Beating cancer was more Girl Scouts, but instead of cookies, you had to sell continuing to live. Instead of badges, you got those pink baseball caps, the ones that all seemed to be for the same team no matter whose logo they printed on them. It was offensive to baseball. Jamie's cancer was vigil cancer, forget-the-color-of-the-ribbon cancer, and would Jamie's blogging be enough to change it to a walking kind? Were words enough? He started posting more photos—him grinning beside an IV drip, the health insurance wedding at City Hall.

"Who's the lucky lady?" wrote Julie, obviously not following the blog closely enough to know that the lucky lady was one former spork. I felt, as a fellow Bestie, that Julie might not be as committed. I emailed, asked what she was doing for the fund-raiser.

"We're making cookies," she wrote. "Me and Rose."

Who the hell was Rose? I hadn't seen her in the comments. There was always another girl, with a name like a flower, coming up right behind your nearest rival to nothing.

I LOOKED for the cookie booth as soon as I arrived. The fund-raiser was in a music hall that liked to throw parties for the season finales of bourgeois television shows. If it was a period drama, people would show up in period costume and pretend to be as hard-drinking as the show's characters. If it was an office comedy, people would wear their most depressing work clothes. At this party, we all dressed as Jamie. I saw the wife right away, wearing the T-shirt, the bracelet, the hoodie, the hat. She'd married into the whole outfit. Julie and her friend were just wearing the T-shirts, tucked into some skirts, but their cookies were warm. Rose asked how I knew Jamie.

"ISTB," I said. I'd coined the blog's abbreviation on the spot. The friend didn't care, was just being friendly behind the baked goods, but Julie was paying attention.

"How do you earn the bracelets?" she asked. I was wearing three.

"He just gives them to his friends."

This was a lie. Everyone got a bracelet. They were in a basket by the door, like condoms.

"Oatmeal raisin brigade!" shouted Jamie. He grabbed a warm cookie without paying, then got into a group hug with all of us.

"These are fantastic," he said. "I'm really glad you came, Captain."

The hug was group, perhaps photo-op group, but inside this hug, his body was alive against my body. New options— divorce, survival—presented themselves. Flash went off and Jamie shook himself out of our hug, gave uploading instructions to the camera guy.

"I didn't make these," I said, to bring him back to the cookie moment. "But I was aware that they were being made."

"You guys are fantastic!" he said, then turned to tell the people who'd made almond bread that they were fantastic. A microphone was being tested, perhaps for karaoke. Someone had spelled out "Jamie Beans for the Cure" with jelly beans.

The whole place had a heady-early-days-of-AIDS feel. Sickness, death, loomed, but the Immuno-Suppress-This-Bitch-a-thon was about concerned members of our community making a difference for one member of our community. Or so Jamie said, thanking us and Big Pharma for keeping him alive, before launching into a rap about kicking Big Pharma's immunosuppressive ass. The rap noted that he was white, to great laughter. Were we laughing because he was white? Because he was sick? Because he was not really a rapper?

"These bracelets are made in China," said someone by the dip. I was drawing patterns in the hummus with a community-garden carrot. I drew a smiley. Someone was willing to call it as they saw it. The bracelets weren't local. They came from the same place that made cancer bracelets for all the cancers. That place was apparently China. The Chinese were manufacturing our hope for the cure. Someone could post this on a blog as evidence of America's decline. People could link to the post, comment on it, then get angry at one another's mutual friends.

The local band was doing sound check. We were all getting ready to like them no matter what, for the fund-raiser. Audience friends nodded and said the last happy thing before a band starts playing, oblivious to the anger they would feel the next day on a comment wall. I saw Jamie, already wrapped around his wife from behind, the vanguard of concert snugglers, the two of them grinning the grins of organizers who appreciate everyone coming out, who've just put their mics back into the mic stand and are now ready to aggressively enjoy music.

Was I being unfair? Who was I to begrudge the terminally ill their right to concert-snuggle smugly? The healthy were wrapped. Man hands above girlfriend hips. I had never gotten to do this, no matter how good the band, but I wasn't maybe dying really soon. Dying was going to take me a while.

The local band made life seem longer. Minutes went by where I wasn't sure if the rest of the music was worth whatever had happened here. Normally in the presence of lack of greatness, I would focus on the bassist's arms, the drummer's shoulders, the differences between their T-shirts, but they were all wearing the same T-shirt. They ended their set by bringing Jamie back onstage and handing him a large guitar. He did the multiple encores we had to ask him for.

"Let's go backstage!" There was Julie in her extra-small tee, wriggling a cancer bracelet over her fingers. I wasn't sure if she wanted Jamie or just the fast friendship of groupie-dom.

"But it's time for the dance-a-thon," I said.

"He said he has something for us," she said.

I pictured bongs with Jamie's face on them, joints with cancer ribbons wrapped around them. I hoped it was pot. I needed perspective.

Julie rushed us past what should have been a bouncer, but was just another girl collecting raffle tickets.

"Thanks," she said, to no one.

We entered a room with mirrors on the ceiling. Guys in the band were dragging their instruments across the floor. Jamie had taken his shirt off. Tattoos I knew well from pictures were right in front of me. A phallic spray of flowers erupted over his shoulder blade. Lupine. I had read about his wildflower identification hobby. His wife was kneading the tattoo like a boxing coach, or a geisha. It was time to give the wife some attention.

"You guys met doing karaoke?" I said. Jamie had told the story of their meeting in his first-date-anniversary blog post and on three different social media sites. Maybe it would be different live.

"I knew I liked her right away," said Jamie, on How We Met

autopilot, but making faces to reflect the effects of the spousal massage. "She could sing. And she was the only woman in Sing It! who didn't seem easy. Some of those girls were desperate."

She smiled wifeishly, dug an elbow into his back.

Was this the reason I found myself alone? I was very easy. I couldn't figure out why to wait. That wasn't it. I could figure out why, but not how. I wasn't ready for someone to think I was the least slutty girl at the bar, to marry what I wouldn't yield.

"Do I seem easy?" I said.

"No," said Jamie. "You're great."

Was great the opposite of easy?

Julie had draped herself over the local drummer. She fed him guacamole. She'd forgotten the mission, our reason for coming backstage, or maybe she was actually interested in the drummer. The wife kept kneading. She dug into Jamie with her fingers, her knuckles, her thumbs.

"Ow!" he yelped. "A little softer, babe. You've got a sick man, here. So I'm diagnosed the morning of our first date. I don't know what to do—do I cancel? Will she think it's an excuse? Having cancer? Somehow I find myself walking to her apartment. I show up at her door with a bouquet of poppies and tell her she probably shouldn't have dinner with me."

They both smiled at this obstacle, quickly overcome because of the wife's determination to accompany him to his entire illness. She was his plus one. I had read this numerous times on ISTB, but the two of them were ready to make people cry in the paper of record. I had friends who were journalists. I could do PR for this cause.

"We can't thank you enough for everything," said the wife. For what? Twenty dollars? IMing her husband at night? Jamie reached around and patted her thigh, massaging the masseuse.

"Maybe I can help more," I said.

. . .

JAMIE HAD a colonoscopy appointment. His wife had to work. I had to work, too, but I'd called in sick, told Jamie and wife that I had the day off. I would be the designated adult to get him after the procedure, or I was designating myself an adult in the presence of a heavily sedated cancer patient I had a crush on. In any event, I was old enough.

Morning light streamed into a pavilion named after somebody wealthy and dead. Nurses wheeled patients through sun motes, patients who didn't bother to squint. A security guard told me I was in the wrong building. These were all the wrong buildings. Not one of them was the right place to be.

I hurried to Outpatient Services, then waited for three hours. I squirted my hands with antibacterial foam. I read a parenting magazine. Before there were blogs, there were magazines. They came every month and told you how to parent as a verb. Now the mommies blogged their mommy screw-ups daily—the burnt nut loaf, the unsafe car seat. They failed publicly to show you they were still people. I wasn't convinced. Jamie's sperm was in a vial somewhere in case his wife needed it later to prove she was still a person. I read this, too, on Jamie's blog. If he made it, he would make a good daddy blogger. If he didn't make it, his children would just whisper their updates, or even dream them. Here in the waiting room, we weren't allowed to use electronic devices to forget where we were. We had to grease up old magazines with our fingers, take advice from outdated horoscopes.

"Who's here for Jamie C.?" A tiny nurse looked for me. My old horoscope had told me to welcome new experiences.

"I'm the designated adult," I said, standing.

"He's in Recovery," she said. I thought the nurse might ask

after Mrs. C., or if she knew Mrs. C., ask why I wasn't her. But she didn't ask. She led me to Recovery, where middle-aged people lay recovering from their routine colonoscopies.

"Can I have my phone, Ida?" said Jamie, once we got behind the curtain. He turned to me. "They let me use it in here."

The nurse handed him the backpack she'd been carrying. It held the clothing he wore to look like the rest of us.

"Don't get dressed too fast," she said. "Or walk out in your shorts like last time."

"I love you, Ida," he said. He took her picture, then my picture, then a picture of the two of us together.

"You're my Champions of the Day," he said. He handed us both stickers out of his bag. "Ida is Champion in Chief. You can be the First Lady."

"I read up on the prep last night," I said, after the departure of the president. "It sounds difficult."

"This is my fifth time," he said. "My shit runs clear before I even drink the stuff."

He didn't look up from his phone as he quipped. He was already typing his impressions of this colonoscopy, comparing it to the previous four.

"I thought you'd be more tired," I said. "Or drugged."

"So you could have your way with me?"

"Of course not," I said. Then I saw that being serious made it seem like I had it worse for him. "I wanted you completely unconscious."

"Well, soon I'll be dead." He smiled and kept blogging.

"What did the doctor say?"

"I only see Singh today. He tells me what he saw. Then Weiselberg calls. She tells me what it means." Weiselberg and Singh were members of the oncology team he kept thanking.

"What could it mean?" I asked.

"Don't you read Immuno?"

"Not that often," I said. "I keep meaning to get around to it."

"I really don't have the energy to catch you up right now. Sorry."

"No, I'm sorry, I'm sorry."

He squinted, then spoke in a new voice.

"I think Julie has a crush on me," he said.

"That's not healthy," I said. Poor Julie. She'd slept with the drummer, but Jamie still suspected her.

"She's all over me. You're all over me. I feel like I can't breathe."

It was confusing to want to punch someone in a hospital gown, but his face above the gown looked like a lot of faces I had seen deliver this message.

"Has the anesthesia worn off?" I asked. Maybe we could blame the drugs.

"Yeah, totally," he said. "People want to be a part of this, and I appreciate that. But I'm married."

"I know you're married. I read your blog."

He looked down, tapped a final set of keys, then sent his words into a sphere all of us used without understanding. We used to call it the World Wide Web, but at some point the world had dropped out. The wide was gone. It was a narrow web connecting us to those who would never love us back.

"I'll let you get dressed." I turned to go to wherever wasn't here.

"No, Captain. Stay for the results."

I stood as far from him as three feet allowed. Jamie put on his clothes. I helped him tie his shoes as a token gesture. Then Singh pulled back the curtain and told us what he saw.

Third Person

REBECCA HAD SEX RECENTLY, but she forgot. The guy had a flat-screen TV in his room, and a brother, who also had a flat screen in his room. There was a third flat screen in the living room for the brothers to watch together.

Rebecca slept with the smaller but older brother. The younger brother looked up from his flat screen as though, Rebecca thought, surprised that his older brother could sleep with a girl as pretty as Rebecca. Later she found out that he only looked surprised because the brother Rebecca slept with actually had a girlfriend. The look was the "You're not his girl-friend" look. Rebecca had seen it before.

Rebecca had seen it this year, when she slept with a bass player, which caused her to get a neck injury and discover a chiropractor. The chiropractor was young and dated another chiropractor. Rebecca left out that the bass player had a girlfriend, because it didn't seem related to her neck. The chiropractor told Rebecca that her problems were in her whole body.

"You can't separate one part of your body from the rest," said the chiropractor. "It turns out they're connected."

Rebecca's insurance covered some of the treatment, but not enough to keep going and find out what was wrong.

The guys with girlfriends never told Rebecca they had girlfriends until after they had slept with her. Maybe they detected some moral strain in her, some impetus to protect girlfriends. Maybe they detected the opposite, and were thus protecting their girlfriends from Rebecca. Rebecca wanted to tell them not to worry, she forgot all the sex she had as soon as she had it, she didn't really have it when she had it, and she hadn't for a long time.

Not That Kind of Sad

THE HOUSEKEEPER is having an affair. My parents talk about her affair when nothing is wrong with the car. When something is wrong with the car, they talk about the car. The car is a Toyota, and the place that fixes the car is also called Toyota. One of my parents drives the Toyota to get fixed while the other follows in the car that is not broken. They drop the Toyota off at Toyota and drive back together in the same car.

The housekeeper says the man is just a friend. My father says there's no way that man is just her friend. My mother says she just hopes the housekeeper is being smart. My grandmother tells my mother the housekeeper wouldn't do it. By "do it," she means "have an affair." My grandmother is around the house all the time. She and the housekeeper speak Spanish with different accents and are friends.

She would do it. She's still doing it. She makes calls from our house. She takes calls at our house. She can only have her affair twice a week, when she cleans our house. I'm in high school, so I don't know why I follow this. I don't have sex. I don't have anything.

The housekeeper has been working at our house for years, but nobody noticed her until she started having an affair. Before that, she was a Jehovah's Witness. It's probably more interesting than what she's doing now.

My grandmother sometimes bakes me a cake after school. She cooks, bakes, and speaks bad English. Sometimes it seems like she is our housekeeper. My grandmother had a husband, but I never met him. He wasn't my grandfather. After he left her, she gained ninety pounds and never left the apartment she lived in in the country she lived in. This took a long time. My mother brought her to our house last year. Nobody talks about when she will leave.

I'm learning to drive. My mother and father argue about whose turn it is to take me out. Teaching me to drive is unpleasant. I'm not ready to face other cars, but they're on the road anyway. In school, we can't be alone in the car with the Driver's Ed teacher. "I'm sure you know why," the teacher says, alluding to a past or future crime. I don't plan to get molested by him. I'm not that kind of sad.

Other kids have housekeepers. When a housekeeper quits, someone's mom will give someone else's mom "a name." "Do you have a name?" "Sheila has a name." There's a network of moms who know women who know how to use a scrub brush, a scouring pad, a sponge mop. The women walk to and from our houses, without Toyotas.

"It's good for them," says my mother.

My mother works with diabetics, so she wants the world to keep its weight down. The housekeeper is not fat but she's not thin. She's the right weight for a husband to start ignoring her and another man to still notice.

My mother tells my father, "If you have an affair, don't bother coming home."

My father laughs. My mother is a pistol from another country, a diabetic counselor. Who would cheat on her? Not my father. It's not smart.

My mother likes the slang from this country, like "SOB" and "POS."

"The husband is probably an SOB," she'll whisper about the housekeeper's husband.

"POS," she'll yell when someone cuts her off.

"Thank God for AC," she'll say in the summer.

Maybe they don't use acronyms in other countries. When I was a kid, we visited my grandmother in her apartment without AC. A useless fan moved air around. The shower took up the whole bathroom, and the toilet was somewhere else. Every time you showered, you had to mop the whole bathroom down the drain. I cried because I had never touched a mop before.

One day the housekeeper gets picked up in a van. I can't see who's driving, her husband or her lover, but I don't know what either of them looks like. She bounces out of our house, so it's probably the lover, or maybe she's just happy to be done making beds for some family to lie in.

I'd like someone to pick me up and take me away. Some kids already drive. They drive their parents' cars or, if they're really rich, their own new cars. They look stupid driving a car they didn't buy. This is America, though. Nobody cares what I think. I doubt my parents will buy me a car, though they will buy me college. I spend most of my time making myself worthy of this purchase. In between studying, I call my one friend, invite her over for a grandmother snack.

"Does she live with you now?" asks the friend, Louisa. My grandmother stands nearby in a hairnet, setting her hair for an event that never takes place.

"No," I say. "I don't think so."

"When is she leaving?"

"Monday," I say.

We eat cake with glasses of milk. Diabetics couldn't have this snack.

"Good cake, Grandma," I shout from the table. "Cake is good."

My grandmother smiles like she understands more than what we say to each other. She rinses some onions to begin dinner preparations. That's a way not to cry. After Monday, I'll say there's a problem with her knees and she has to stay longer to see American doctors. It's true that there is a problem with her knees, long-running. She can't really walk, and gets driven by my mother to Weight Watchers and to have hair electrolysized off her chin. If I learn to drive, I can take over these errands. It's very motivating.

"My dad's mom is more of a regular grandma type," I say. "She belongs to a golf club."

"I hate golf," says Louisa.

We have no time for golf. After this snack is over, we have to study together, which means Louisa shares her flash cards with me. As disciplined as I am, I cannot bring myself to make my own flash cards. I feel something like guilt, but I've already paid her in cake. I'm set for flash cards for the foreseeable future.

My mother comes into my room and offers us grapes on a tiny plate.

"We're full," I say. "We're quizzing each other."

"A plethora of snacks at your house," says Louisa, practicing flash card words. "I like it here."

"I'd prefer the snack wasn't cake," says my mother, but she can't control what gets baked. Her mother is her mother. That's the reason she gives my father for why my grandmother stays. My father seems ready for it to just be our family and the people who clean for our family again. My grandmother is not his family. His mother is where she belongs, eating her meals on a golf course.

The next day I get home from school and my grandmother is not there. I wonder if she's left for good, if they took her to the airport and nobody told me. But her things are still in the basement, her housecoat, her shoes. The basement smells like her. She has sisters and brothers who smell like her, too. My grandmother was one of twelve. A few have died, but a lot are still left. They assist dentists or sell tools to dentists. My grandmother was the oldest and didn't get to go to dental assistant school because she was needed at home.

Where is she now? She could have gone grocery shopping, walked very slowly to the Dairy Barn to buy the cream she whips for my strawberries. I wait an hour. I eat rice cakes with nothing else. I call both parents and reach neither. I call the housekeeper's number on the refrigerator. A man answers.

"Is Isobel home?" I say.

"She cleans today," he says.

"She's not cleaning here today," I say. "I can't find my grandmother, and I thought maybe they went somewhere together. Sometimes Isobel drives her to the pool."

"Isobel don't have a car."

"Right," I say. I remember the van out front, sense he's not its driver. "They take a taxi. From here. Isobel walks to our house and then they take a taxi to the pool. Swimming's good exercise for old people."

"Call the swimming pool," he says, and hangs up.

Both my grandmother and the housekeeper are not where they're supposed to be. They've escaped. I call my mother again. Her secretary says she's left for the day due to a family emergency.

"I am her family."

"Oh, I didn't recognize your voice. Your grandmother, honey. She's in stable condition, but she was struck by a car crossing the street this afternoon."

"Shit," I say. It's not a flash card word, but something new I'm practicing.

"They're at St. Joseph's."

I have no way to get to St. Joseph's. Now my father calls and tells me to stay put. He says my grandmother crosses the street like a turtle. He says that she has been "banged up a bit," but once she's healed, it will be time for her to go home. By home, he doesn't mean here. I tell him Isobel's been lying about cleaning our house to have her affair. I tell him I don't care, but I thought he should know.

"We'll worry about that later," he says, as though there will be a family meeting to decide what to do.

"How will Grandma get around after she goes back?" I say. "Will she still go to Weight Watchers?"

"It's an international organization," he says.

I call Louisa, tell her that we may have to study at her house from now on.

"I hope you like celery," she says. "My mother doesn't want me getting fat."

"I like celery," I say. I like most things. It's something my parents have always valued about me. I look in the fridge to see what remains. Yesterday's cake, outlined in foil. The grapes we should have eaten instead. Cheese, which people eat for breakfast, lunch, and dinner in the country where my grandmother lives. I don't know what they eat in the housekeeper's country or in the country of her lover. Probably cheese.

The doorbell rings. Some kids' doorbells make a song, but my parents probably never got that far in the doorbell catalog. They keep it simple—one kid, two sedans. Vans are for moms to drive around a brood, or for lovers who have to make deliveries. But there's no van parked out front. Through the window, I see a man who looks as afraid of me as I feel of him. Without hearing his voice, I know it's Isobel's husband. We're the ones stuck waiting for everyone else to come home.

It Doesn't Have to Be a Big Deal

THE POT GROWER WAS BROKE. I paid for everything. We went to a restaurant funded by someone else's pot money that served only the kind of food you'd eat when you had the munchies—hamburgers wrapped in mango, zucchini pop tarts. It was hard to date a grower without money. Something had happened to his crop, something dumb. It had to do with his ex-girlfriend, an older woman who threw eggs at his car while we were eating in the munchie restaurant. When we came out, the car said "Faggot" in ChapStick and he was like, "I'm surprised she would write that. She has so many gay friends."

The car also said "Douche bag."

I had never really dated anyone. Sometimes I wondered if a pot grower was the place to start. A lot of his sentences began, "When I had money," and ended with guitars I'd never heard of. We drove back to his grow house with egg dripping off the side of the car, then fucked in an Aeron chair he'd bought when he had money.

Afterward he disappeared behind a duct-taped curtain to tend the plants that would make new guitars possible. I walked around his block, which looked like suburbia as imagined by stoners who had dropped out of college. It was. They had. The college was in the center of town and the dropouts thrived around it, growing richer than if they had finished. My drop-out had become an exception to this rule. The growers grew vegetables, too—rhubarb, kale. I looked for the ex-girlfriend's house. She could be anywhere, seething with misplaced homophobia, cradling intact eggs.

The whole town smelled like pot. Why was he broke? There was weed in his freezer. There was weed in ceramic frogs on his desk. When I tried to smoke a bowl with even a tiny bit of ash in it, he would refill the bowl immediately.

"I want you to smoke fresh," he said.

He propped up my neck with pillows when my neck hurt. He propped up my crotch with pillows to enter me at pillow-propped angles. He seemed neither faggot nor douche bag, but more like a man with a lot of pillows.

The ChapStick wouldn't come off the windshield. The grower scrubbed and scrubbed. We were taking a road trip to a naked hot spring, but he kept pulling over at gas stations and using the squeegee on "Faggot." I blamed his Catholicism, his upbringing. Hippies always had parents.

"It's off, for Christ's sake," I said. I hoped Christ would help. In my religion, he wasn't the son of God. "Just a man," they told us. He was just a man.

"Roll me one," said the grower.

"While you're driving?"

I wasn't from California, so a lot of this was new to me, the pot culture, the nudity without shame. I liked being stoned and naked with this man, but being sober and clothed was more challenging. We had met the previous summer, felt each other up during a sing-along, and decided through emoticon-heavy negotiations that I would fly across the country so we could spend a week together. I sent pictures of myself in a bikini, chaste for our era, but I had a thing about keeping my actual boobs a surprise. He sent pictures of himself playing mandolin in a new band, chubbier than I remembered, his hair in pigtail buns and braids, hair I was excited to overlook in order to like him.

"It doesn't have to be a big deal" was my mantra, or what my friends gave me as a mantra, or what the culture gave us as a mantra, the culture of managing your mantras.

"You can just have fun."

"It can just be for fun."

"It will be really fun."

Was it fun? I learned a lot about his recent struggles as a bluegrass musician. I learned that the bluegrass community was not as big as it was years ago, when that movie with the bluegrass sound track came out.

"It was pretty influential," he said. "Now everything is computers."

Former bandmates had turned to electronica, left the area, died.

"After Dano had the accident, Rob sold all his instruments and headed to Hawaii," he said, reviving a conversation we'd already had several times at his house. I thought of it as the "I'm mad at Dano for dying in a car crash and breaking up the band but I can't admit it so I'll resent Rob instead" loop. I guess he thought we'd try the conversation in the car. I still had no idea how to respond, except to say it was a shame to lose someone so young. Then he said his new band had stronger musicians anyway and put on their CD. The new band sounded just like the old band. All bluegrass sounded the same to me.

"None of us knew if Turkey Flower would stay together, but for Rob to just go . . ." The grower looked at the road, baked out of his mind, trying to understand.

I could have probed the Dano anger, but I didn't want to talk about Dano either. I had enough of my own grief. I couldn't make room for a twenty-four-year-old grower who had bashed his van into a traffic median. Dano had played everything I asked for at the sing-along. He had been cheating on his girlfriend, who was now his widow. Rob had gone to bed early the night we all sang together, resting up for his big betrayal.

"At least you have a fun job," I said. "I just tutor dyslexic teens for standardized tests."

"The way my business is, it's not going to last," he said. "We're in a sweet spot right now with the medical permits."

Cigarette companies were already buying up the land we were speeding past for the day pot became legal.

"To put the little guy out of business," he said. "I guess I'm the little guy."

He was a big guy, with a vengeful ex-girlfriend, in a hundred fifty dollars debt to me. The hot spring would cost twenty-five each for day use. But we had to do things. Otherwise, it wasn't an experience. It was just sitting in his house.

"I understand why Gretchen's mad," he said, eyeing a vague smear on the windshield. "She's not a bad person. She could be really sweet."

"I haven't had a chance to see that side of her," I said.

I hadn't really dated anyone, but I had also not really dated everyone. Without a Gretchen of my own, I began to tell him about the other men. I made them seem like SAT words—this one had been impetuous, that one reclusive. My hope was to stir the pot grower to greater vocab scores.

"What a fool," he offered. "That guy sounds like a jerk."

"I don't know why I'm telling you about him. He was nothing. He's engaged."

We pulled into a wooded lot and parked next a bulletin board that said "We Are a Clothing Optional Resort." The springs steamed behind wet steps. Kiosk notices alerted us to internecine management conflicts, meditation workshops, the healing power of lithium. Women walked by with breasts that left you feeling conflicted. Testicles dangled. I had never even been to a hot spring with bathing suits. The grower went to the bathroom while I purchased day passes with my SAT earnings.

"It's explained in the guidebook, but these are holy waters," said the guy at the front desk. He had a half-shaved head and a T-shirt that said "Question Male Privilege." He handed me a guidebook as thick as a course packet. "So we prefer you not speak, eat, or engage in sexual congress. No passion in the pools."

We undressed in the locker room. A man rocked a woman gently in the water. A sign reminded us to be silent at all times. Sexual activity was not permitted, but the attempts to hide it were worse.

The grower and I began communicating in hot spring sign language.

Over there. I'm going over there.

Okay. I'm staying here.

His hair was longer wet.

You look like Jesus, I signed, pointing to his hair and making the sign of the cross.

He got it, smiled, gave me a wet hug. This was what it was

for, dating. Wet hugs. Jesus jokes. I needed this. I would get high and have this.

I was paying for it. The weed he gave me started to even things out, but I estimated that we had only smoked a hot spring's day pass worth of weed so far.

Smoke? I mimed. I lit an imaginary bubbler.

A woman put her finger to her lips, though we were not talking. Maybe the Original Mantra was "Shush." I judged her breasts as revenge, but they weren't bad by naked hot spring standards. In the southern part of the state, bodies were tanned and injected to perfection, but here in the north, where we bathed, bodies relaxed and gave in to an idea of perfect acceptance. Signs advertised workshops to reclaim powers long forgotten. People banged drums in the parking lot, unlocked childhood trauma in sacral tissue, painted their penises with raspberries.

I checked out his penis—not hard. This was also what dating was for, to see the penis at rest. It rested out of politeness to the naked strangers, so as not to disturb their patented water massage techniques, or maybe it rested out of guilt. I didn't understand the mechanism of control behind the penis, though I respected it. I didn't understand the mechanism of control behind Catholicism either, or behind any of the Eastern religions represented in the hot spring course packet.

We found a clearing in the woods, known around here as the Garden of Peace. He produced a bubbler from its velveteen satchel. We smoked under a Navajo quote. "Thoughts are like arrows: once released, they strike their mark."

"More like Garden of Cultural Appropriation," I said. This was one of the phrases you got to keep if you had not dropped out of college.

"Cultural appropriation," he said. He tasted it on his tongue, added it to his worldview. We were sitting on a rock naked. I felt like a tutor with a promising student at the beginning of time.

"A lot of those Native quotes are made up," he said.

"Everything's made up," I said.

He edged closer to me on the rock. This was my favorite kind of sex, sex based on being impressed. We kissed like we'd been kissing for days, like it was important, like something bad would happen if we stopped.

He lifted a condom out of the velveteen satchel. I checked the label to see if it was flavored. He'd bought a variety pack by accident and some of the condoms smelled like strawberries. Even high, I refused to accept a flavor in my vagina. A condom should be condom flavored, not try to appropriate fruit. Things should be what they were. But what were they?

"It's coconut."

"That's not okay."

He looked for another one, then dumped out the whole satchel. Soon we were surrounded by condoms, the ones that stimulated, the ones that delayed stimulation. One, suspiciously, promised "a swirl."

"I'll just blow you," I said.

I fell back on the blow job when flummoxed. The guys I hadn't really dated hadn't really minded, but this guy, this grower, he wanted to connect. He wanted eye contact, he wanted smiles.

"This is nice," I kept saying.

Like a hooker, eye contact and hand-holding had become a bigger deal to me than sex itself. Except I wasn't paid not to have feelings. I had broken my own spirit for free.

"Look at me," he said, while I was sucking him. Had Gretchen maintained eye contact throughout? Were two and a half years of fellatio eye contact the reason he had left her in charge of his crop at a crucial moment during the weed harvest while he went on tour in central Oregon with his bluegrass duo?

I looked at him. But there was someone coming up behind him. The guy from the front desk ducked under a dream catcher and grabbed my grower's shoulder. I pulled my mouth off the penis like I had tasted something lychee flavored. I couldn't stop being naked, so I laid one arm across my breasts and fanned the other hand over my crotch.

"The guidelines were clearly stated at the front desk," he said. "I'm sorry, man, but you and your lady friend are going to have to leave the Garden of Peace."

"We're very sorry, sir," I said. "Would you mind if we still used the tubs?"

I made eye contact with the guy from the front desk. Suddenly I was good at eye contact. Something was bubbling up in me, my upbringing. We had paid for day use. I had never been kicked out of anything. The guy from the front desk had only the authority of being the lone clothed person here.

After Adam and Eve were kicked out of the garden, could they still use the tubs? Biblical scholars were divided.

"We'll be good," I said, trying to stick out my tits while keeping them covered.

"I can't know that," said God. He had seen a lot of tits.

"We paid for day use, sir," I said. "*I* paid."

I was trying a new biblical approach—Eve with earning power, Eve without shame. Now Adam (formerly Jesus) stood, newly flaccid, walked away from the rock, and began flipping over Tibetan prayer flags on a string at the edge of the garden. He was either too stoned to be embarrassed or was so embarrassed that he was pretending to be extremely stoned.

"Alright, I have to get back to the front desk." Our interloper ran his fingers through the side of his head that still had hair. "The tubs are open for another half hour, so please be mindful of the other bathers."

God left us in the Garden of Cultural Appropriation.

"We get to stay!" I said. "In general!"

"I'm going to pay you back," said the grower. He was putting the pipe away. He was gathering Trojans.

I waved my hand as though money was no object. I wanted to stay in general.

"As soon as Rob gets back from Hawaii," he said. "I'll be able to get it to you then."

"What does this have to do with Rob?"

"He owes me three thousand dollars."

"Jesus. You lent him that much? What's he doing there?"

"He's apprenticing with craftsmen who make ukuleles."

"No doubt he'll have the money, then," I said. "Maybe when Rob gets back, he can tell us whether tropical-fruit-flavored condoms are big in Hawaii."

The grower muttered something about the variety pack being on sale.

Had I been brought up to be a jerk? Now I had a new number in my head, the amount owed me as a percentage of what Rob owed. It could be an SAT question. The thought stayed in my head as we dipped back into a pool with wrinkle-tanned old people in excellent health. Be us, their bodies seemed to say. Our penises only work intermittently, but our hearts are full.

My tits were going to fall. My eggs would dry up, or run out. I didn't really know what happened to eggs. I wondered if Gretchen had run out. I wondered if Gretchen had had an abortion, and then I knew she'd had an abortion. That's what couples went through together in order to hate each other later for the right reasons. That's why he didn't know about the plain condoms. They were a secret for people who used birth control consistently.

We still had three days left together. I thought of asking him to drive me to the airport. I'd leave him enough money to get him home. The airport was four hours away, though, and changing my ticket would be another fee. But going back with him had costs, too—dinner, gas, condoms, lube. Maybe we'd get egged again.

How much did a ukulele cost? I wanted to be someone's girlfriend, not their creditor. What would Jesus do? Would Jesus lend a friend three thousand dollars? Of course he would. Would Jesus' girlfriend ask for two hundred dollars back? This wasn't my culture.

He wrapped his leg around mine underwater, then opened his mouth to speak illegally.

"Just be a little patient with me," he said.

That wasn't my culture, either. I could cultivate patience, lean against his chest in a tub of hot volcano water, silently workshop my anger, learn more about Rob's craftsmanship. Or I could go. I couldn't decide which would be a bigger deal.

Phyllis

A FAMILY filmed themselves, but only on vacation.
The grandchildren have the Super 8 reels transferred to digital. They watch with their grandmother Phyllis.

"Everyone was always swimming," say the children. "Grandma, you had a body."

"I was quite thin," says Phyllis.

Phyllis isn't fat, just old. Phyllis lifts weights at a gym called Midtown. She is the oldest person at the gym. They feature her in the gym's newsletter, *Alive*. Midtown is not in the real Midtown. The gym is in upstate New York, and so is Phyllis.

THE FAMILY never films themselves moving, but they move, farther and farther up the state, because of the father's job, until the mother, Phyllis, says she won't move again unless it's in a box. The family stays still. Then the father, Eugene, dies. Phyllis, a social worker, advances to therapist. Eugene doesn't leave much and she needs to earn to pay the mortgage, to foot the gym bills, to afford her therapist scarves.

Phyllis goes to self-esteem conferences in Canada. She stands on the Great Wall of China. She makes friends on an elder tour in France, where the guide holds up reproductions of Monet's "Water Lilies" in front of real water lilies, to prove Monet was there.

Phyllis brings back dolls you can't get in the United States anymore. She brings back visors that say "Galapagos Islands." She brings back Swedish chocolates, Portuguese tiles, Oaxa-can skulls. She brings back tiny Peruvian finger puppets, and makes you wear them.

Phyllis redecorates. Buddhas appear where there had hith-erto been no Buddhas. Mirrored wallpaper gets torn down and replaced with mirrored walls. Phyllis needs to see herself in every direction. Picture Phyllis.

Phyllis is a shrink, but she is also shrinking. Osteoporosis does not stop her. She builds muscle, replaces hips, replaces cars.

Phyllis's hair starts brown, but soon an upstate colorist con-vinces Phyllis that red would be fun. Upstate, red means fun.

Phyllis's hairdresser dyes Phyllis's daughter's hair red from the same color swatch. Her daughter lives nearby so her chil-dren can attend the schools that Phyllis's taxes make great. Phyllis can't tell her son to dye his hair red, too, because he is a man and because he doesn't live upstate anymore. As a young man, this son took out a road map of the United States and drew a circle with a five-hundred-mile radius around the town where Phyllis lived. He put states in between him and Phyllis, several mountain ranges, a river.

Phyllis warned him: If he goes, the family will forget him. Not one of them will recognize his face when he comes back for a visit. "Mark?" they'll say. "Who?" If he goes, it will kill his sister. It will kill his father, who is already dead.

"I guess I'm only the mother," sighed Phyllis, at the airport.

Phyllis's son lives the rest of his life outside the radius. He studies Mark Twain (his favorite Mark), the Impressionists, and a staggering amount of biology. He beds the women of Boston, Toronto, Tel Aviv, weds a woman of Rio de Janeiro, puts his children in a New Jersey school system. He films his children with a VHS camera. They're in bathing suits. They're going to visit Grandma Phyllis. Video cameras get smaller. Grandma Phyllis gets smaller. Then Mark's life starts ending. This too gets filmed. The family's in a fancy restaurant with a waterfall because why not? What are they saving it for? Someone films the waterfall.

Phyllis belts, "Mark needs hospice care" into the phone to her daughter, brags about how she has correctly predicted organ failure before: Eugene's colon, Bernice's kidney. Now this. She remembers her sister Bernice on dialysis, Bernice gone, Bernice nothing. What luck to have a nephrologist in the family. What luck. Phone calls.

The nephrologist is Phyllis's daughter with the same red hair. She lives five minutes away from Phyllis for thirty years. A quick car ride in case of emergency. They know each other's alarm codes. The alarms call the police. But that never happens. Nothing happens except Phyllis letting herself into her daughter's house and punching the code before the end of thirty seconds. Phyllis has the keys.

Phyllis can't sleep. She keeps the radio on all night, watches musicals about riverboats, state fairs. She is having insomnia from the 1940s. She has lost a husband, a father, a sister, a son. Her mother, Elsie, is a story for another day. Elsie was a health-food nut before it was the custom, in addition to being regular nuts. She snacked on seeds and turned out to be right about red meat. Now Phyllis eats chocolate, only chocolate— chocolate-flavored rice cakes, chocolate éclairs, chocolate-shaped Freud (a gift from a patient), and she can't sleep. At 4:30 a.m. she drives to Midtown, treads the elliptical, handles the lady weights, gossips about her grandchildren, the careers they refuse to have in spite of doing well in their respective school systems.

Then Phyllis, too, dies. They run an obit in *Alive*. Personal trainers testify to her indomitable spirit.

$$F = ma$$

THE WAY THEY CHEATED was with calculators. Half the questions on the tests came straight from the homework. One boy figured out the answers and put them in the other boys' calculators in exchange for friendship. The boy who knew the answers was very short, almost as short as me, a short girl. He had to shave every day starting early, though—he was that kind of short. I'm the other kind, the kind that had to shave late. I did everything late. I'm still waiting for a lot of things to happen to me.

The blind man lived near me. He was my neighbor. I would see him walking home in his suit and cane. He wasn't totally blind. He could see a little bit. He graded our tests on a large-print screen. One letter, one number, took up the whole screen. I went into his office after I failed the first test and saw my answer up there on the screen, big and wrong.

$F = ma$

The boys would meet at the house of the boy who knew the answers, and they were all boys. I was the only girl in the class except for a girl who didn't talk. The blind man thought I was the only girl in the class. He told me there were a lot of smart boys in that class and I would have to work extra hard to keep up, but I knew that there was only one smart boy in the class and he was giving the other boys the answers. So I left the blind man a note. I don't know how he read it, if he had a magnifying glass or if his wife read it to him, but the next time we weren't allowed to use those calculators.

The boys who weren't smart failed. They didn't cry. They groaned boy groans and gave the smart boy a wedgie. He took the wedgie and went to MIT on a scholarship. I began to cheat using tiny scraps of paper. I made new friends.

Rate Me

THE AD SAID "I will rate your vagina," so I sent it in. It got a two. Warts.

They sent it back with the warts removed. At a doctor's office, uninsured, the procedure would have cost an arm and a leg. I sent those in, too. My raters shaved my legs and spray-tanned them. They won't tan anymore in the real sun.

My face got a four point five.

My second face got a six. My raters rated my parts in a converted strip mall by the sea. They hung up a sign that said "Rate Me" over a sign that had said "Oceanside Shoe Repair." Also, it was more than just rating. They laid cool cloth across my brow, extracted blackheads, taught me that my armpits might be expendable. They trimmed split ends. They dyed my hair.

"Who needs armpits, girl?" I said to a man applying foil packets to my head.

"I'm straight," he said.

"Can I ask you out, then?"

"I'd prefer you didn't do that," he said. "My last date with a face was a disaster. A nine, but when she climaxed, a low seven."

WHAT CONSTITUTED PERFECTION? Nobody at Rate Me would explain. They sent back my arms with a long rubric—softness, muscle tone, strokeability. I had low squeeze factor, a weak hug. My rater advised practice with friends or family members before I advanced to hugging members of the gender that scared me.

MY FEET actually had a good shot at a ten, though the toenail fungus was a problem. I treated the yellow nails with a polish, prescribed by the famous in-house doctor, Dr. Rater. Dr. Rater had founded RateMyMD, and Do You Think I'm a Hypochondriac??? Girls with lupus, fibromyalgia, questionable freckles, gathered in a former sporting goods warehouse, eyed the white coat, grew new moles on the spot. Dr. Rater made a show of not taking advantage.

MY VAGINA couldn't break five. I consulted with a vulva adviser, who told me, "I haven't seen this much bush since I went to uni." He wasn't Australian, either. He was Something American, his ancestors had once peddled shoes, and he wasn't afraid to hurt a client's feelings. Body hair in unwanted areas was an easy fix, according to Rate Me's brochures. Rate Me eschewed razors and wax—too messy—and went straight for the latest in radiation hair removal. When I got my vagina back from them, rated, irradiated, they'd put it in a satin box with a note telling me that I was now eligible to dine with other top-rated members, and a gift card that said "Ratings Addict."

"WHY ARE YOU DOING THIS?" asked my friend with self-confidence.

"I want to improve," I said. "I want my vagina to improve."

She didn't bother handing me a vagina mirror or making me read a self-confidence book. She had too much confidence for that. If we'd been reversed, and she'd been sending her nose to get evaluated, I would have gotten her a book, talked to her about talking to someone besides me.

"I need therapy," I said. "But without insurance, I can't really afford it."

"You know you're great," she said in a depressed voice. "You should stop worrying about your pores and start reading again."

"I read. My pores are enlarged, but I read."

"I read, too," she said.

YOU COULD USE A GIFT CARD for a plasty. Rhinoplasty. Labiaplasty. The surgeon's catalog showed ten after perfect ten. Puffed labia were yesterday's labia. Today's labia dipped in. A group of raters resigned over the gift cards. They left a note tacked to a kiosk that said "Plastic surgeons are BUYING your raters off. Those of us who went into the rating profession to let women know the truth about themselves are disgusted and saddened by the corrupt influence of these so-called doctors. To that end, we must bid you sevens adieu. We're starting a company called Natural Ratings for women who find beauty in the way they were born but still want to be a better version of themselves for the sense of well-being being better brings."

"One-to-ten is done," they added. "We're switching to a five-star system."

The note stayed up for weeks, but the man who did my highlights never came back. I thought about calling him up, but I didn't want stars. That would make me feel like a restaurant.

MY BREASTS got an eight. That was a surprise, considering their average buoyancy. I wondered if one of my raters was getting soft on me. Maybe he was into me now, the speed at which my appendages shipped, the re-taped box, the packing peanuts. Maybe he just liked nipple hair. I like it. We have to stay sentimental about one flaw, coddle our attachment to something, so we can do extreme violence to the rest. It's like how the president has a dog.

"ARE YOU CRAZY?" asked my mother.

"I have to live my life," I said.

"Rate your life," said my mother. She left messages saying she was just calling to say hi, but when I called back, it was always more than that.

MY NIPPLES came back bruised. Someone had been gnawing on them.

I held for an operator while an automated voice asked me to rate my call so far. The operator, when I reached her, said that she would strive to address my concerns to the best of her abilities. I told her my concerns. The operator said that Rate Me could not be held responsible for damages incurred during the shipping process. Also, might I consider electrolysis on my nipples? They had a guy. He was very good.

"Packages don't bite nipples," I said. "And don't women over there do anything besides answer phones? Women have broken into electrolysis in the non-rating world."

The operator assured me that she had many job responsibilities, then asked if I wanted the truth about my ass. I didn't want it yet. An ass rating meant new skirts to hide flaws, or to show off the ass you didn't even know you were hiding. I had already let the Rate My Wardrobe people into my closet. They let women do the closet, or at least hold the trash bag.

"You could be an operator-rater," I said to the operator. "You could rate voices. Voices are underrated."

"Silence, too," she said. "I'm going to need you to hold for just a moment while I fetch a supervisor."

"No, wait, Linda, don't bother. I'm terminating my membership, effective immediately."

I had no idea if her name was Linda, but saying "effective immediately" made me feel strong. I had quit dating sites with the same terminology. I had stopped wilderness catalogs from coming to my home.

"Rate Me is sorry to see you go," she said. "We thought parts of you had potential."

World Trade Date

SHE WENT ON DATES with guys who'd been there. They seemed to be doing a lot of dating, the ones who'd escaped, and claimed to be humbled, but they were usually as humble as guys who hadn't been there. The only ones humbled were the ones who hadn't escaped, maybe, but they were out of the dating pool. She felt sorry for her dates, regardless. It seemed sad that to sit in a bar with her was what you did when you got your life back.

You also moved to Brooklyn. You got your life back in Brooklyn. Guys who had designed web pages in or near there left to design web pages in Brooklyn. One of them showed her his pages. He had designed for a bakery, a congressional aide, an aunt. They looked at his pages for two hours, then had intercourse.

"I had a really nice time," he said.

She and another guy got a ticket for trespassing by the river to watch the sun set over what was no longer there.

"I would have never done this before," said the guy, as they climbed through a hole in a fence about to be gentrified out of having holes.

She was grateful to the cop for interrupting the sunset, any requirements it might have had. The guy told the cop there should be a sign. The cop sighed. He handed them each a summons and pointed to the fence.

"In New York State," he said, "your fence is your sign."

Had the cop been there? If he'd been there, he probably wouldn't be here, explaining their summonses.

"You take the morning off from work and go to this address," said the cop. "Just tell the judge you were watching the sunset with your friend. Maybe he's having a good day. I respect that it's a beautiful night, but after what happened, we can't take any chances. If you don't go to this address by December first, you could be arrested at a later date. You could have been arrested right now."

"Thank you," they said.

The cop got back in his cop car, rolled away, alive.

"Prick," said the guy.

SHE WASN'T some trauma groupie. She attended no vigils, contributed to no quilts. She wasn't looking for it, but if a friend said, "I have a friend. He was there. He just moved to Brooklyn," she would give her friend permission to let the guy put her number into his device. Then bar, sunset, web pages, intercourse.

One guy, Steve, took her to breakfast the next day. They walked blocks and blocks, holding hands in a determined way.

He told her he had gotten back with his girlfriend after it happened. He was still back with his girlfriend.

Steve's breakfast place had teddy bears for sadness. One of the teddy bears was wearing a fireman slicker, holding a hose. It was a hero. It was rescuing Eggs Benedict. She ordered the Florentine. There was sort of an altar for these bears. People left flowers for the bears, candy for the bears, bears for the bears.

She didn't want to be remembered. People said you lived on in memory, but she knew that being remembered definitely meant you were dead. Steve finished his toast. He told her that he'd had a really nice time.

WHY WERE THEY all having such a nice time? Weren't they supposed to not call her again? They were all calling again. The ticket guy wanted to go to court with her. Web Pages wanted to take her to his aunt's bakery. The bakery was having a sale on flag marzipan. They would make your loved one's missing poster into a cake.

No, she canceled. She was sick, she was busy, she was really sick and busy. It was one thing to go on a blind date, quite another to go when you had actually seen the person. She'd pay the fine herself, get her cupcakes somewhere unaffiliated.

But everywhere was affiliated. If not bears, it was collages. If not collages, it was handprint murals from kindergarten classes in states that would be boring to attack. Her office rented a therapist, even though everybody already had their own therapist. The subway told her it was okay to get help, even if you weren't there when it happened, even if you were in Machu Picchu when it happened. She couldn't pass a corner without a shrine, a fence that wasn't tricked out with Xeroxes of the dead. Bears got wet in the rain. The dead looked deader Xeroxed.

She asked her dates if they knew anybody on the fences. They never did.

"Different company," they'd sputter. "Different floor."

"But maybe you saw them in the elevator, in the lobby, by the snack machine?"

"Our company had its own snack machine."

HER COMPANY didn't have a snack machine. Her company locked its bathroom "for security reasons" and left the keys in the receptionist's mug. The mug had a picture of the receptionist's grandson on it, graduating from something. She went to the bathroom a lot at work. The keys were sometimes a little warm, a little wet. Once she forgot the keys in the bathroom, and the receptionist had to call security to unlock what had locked behind her. Nobody would bomb the bathroom, she felt certain. It was too big a hassle.

Other offices made you wear a laminated ID tag, and some guys would forget to take off their laminated ID tags when they arrived to meet her at street corners, or on museum steps. The museum was a creative date, and a poor idea. She liked to be on a barstool, perched and ready to judge. She'd look from a guy's face to the face hanging from his neck, a face that could be on a fence, but wasn't.

Another Cake

THEY CAME EVERY DAY with their prayer books and coconut candies. Every day they came, careful not to slip on the driveway—*it's icy*—offering cold cheeks for a kiss. My aunts took their coats, their cakes. I took their sorries, then hid in my old room. There wasn't much to look at: mirror shrouded in a bath towel, a poster of the Beatles crossing the street, bits of Fun-Tak where sunflowers and revolutionaries had been, blue bits like mold on the white wall. The bookshelf was half empty, just a French-English dictionary and some young adult paperbacks. I reread the one about the gawky girl who loses her virginity to the paraplegic genius, the one about the southern toughie who's beaten by her step-dad and rubs herself against a pillow imagining she's on fire. The southern one was listed as a finalist for a major award, but I had dog-eared the rubbing pages and forgotten the rest of the story. This was not the

South. This was New Jersey and there were people downstairs, clustered around fruit baskets.

The people made noises. Doorbell noises. Flushing noises.

"Sloan Kettering," they whispered, the way they whispered "Harvard."

"Stage four," they said, like an SAT score.

I slipped my father's old LPs onto the turntable: "Let It Be," "Desire." I made weeping noises. The guests chomped cheddar cheese. On day three, I took a shovel to the driveway to break up the ice. Someone, my mother said, could fracture a hip and sue. I gripped the shovel with my father's enormous gloves, then swung it in circles over my head before bringing it down on what could become litigation. Those driving by might have mistaken me for a midget dad gone berserk. He'd had it with mortgage installments and the Temple Brotherhood. Take that, frozen water. Only my father hadn't joined the Brotherhood. We weren't big on joining. He refused to sign me up for Brownies, though I wanted more than anything to march through the cafeteria with those brown shirts. I wanted a badge.

Maybe if he had been a Temple Brother, we wouldn't have had such a hard time finding a rabbi to officiate the funeral. Years before, on one of my parents' evening walks, my father had mentioned to my mother that he wanted to be cremated when he died. He didn't like the idea of his body rotting underground.

My mother listened, though she had assumed they would be laid to rest alongside each other, in the final conjugal bed.

"I worry about being cold," she said.

"You won't feel it."

Plates were scraped, tomato sauce slid into garbage bags. I inserted the quadratic formula while my parents circled the subdivision on foot. Where did they go? What did people in cars think? We didn't even have the pretense of a dog. Then off to college—Nietzsche, penetration.

"Daddy said he wanted cremation. What do you think?"

Suddenly, my mother and I were married. Husband's dead? Meet your new husband. Standing tall at five foot two, your new husband is majoring in Cultural Studies and has recently become sexually active. What did I think?

We had him cremated, against Jewish law, and somehow I was put in charge of convincing a rabbi to not bury him. I made phone calls. I hoisted the Bergen County Yellow Pages onto the kitchen counter. I argued that I had been bat mitzvahed at Temple Beth Fill-In-the-Blank, that I had danced with my father at Fill-In, that my father had taken my bony wrists and spun me out and back in front of laughing, clapping friends of the family.

No rabbi found this story moving. No rabbi would touch it. They were all too afraid of the Board, the unseen uglies behind the temple throne, just waiting for a kashrut scandal or an opportunity to give out pens. Finally, we imported a guy from Westchester County, and at this point I don't know why we bothered, because he was obviously some kind of third-rate rabbi, and he smiled waxily when he met me, grateful to have the gig.

THE FUNERAL HOME DIRECTOR told my mother, my aunts, and me to wait in the back office of Diforio Memorial. We would be called out when everyone was seated. Rows of brown metal chairs stood stacked against one wall, and behind them someone had hung a sheet over a giant cross. The outline of the cross was still visible, the hiding perfunctory, as though the funeral home director had applied the "If the Deceased Is Jewish" section from the mortician's instruction manual. I stared at my father's sisters as they asked the rabbi pointless logistical questions, a frenzy in black suits. How did they know to own them? Nothing could stop them from putting on pantyhose or a gold bracelet, not even death.

That morning, my aunt Susan had reached into the bottom of her divorcée suitcase, past balls of stockings and cream-colored underwear, and tossed me a pair of tights. Sternly, like she was trying to teach me a lesson. The underwear chilled me, with its connotations of the aunt's lonely crotch, under-served by the male divorcés in her area. I wondered if the rabbi was single. Maybe she could date him. The rabbi had thick lips, and a tie the color of lox. All morning, I kept thinking about eating the tie. Maybe we would get to have lox after we had returned to the house, where everything would smell like onions and cleaning fluid. Oh, there would be lox. Some woman would make it appear, and then she would disappear, so the lox would appear to have appeared on its own.

"The best thing about being Jewish," the rabbi kidded us, "is that we keep our funerals short."

Aunt Susan laughed conspiratorially, like you wouldn't believe what her Taoist friends had put her through.

I turned to eye-roll with my mother, who had always com-plained that Susan was a flirt. But my mother was staring at me.

"What?" I said.

I knew what. My nipples were poking at my dress. There's not much to do about pokey nipples, to be honest, except try to warm them so they flatten. But if you rub them, they might get pokier.

"Do you want my jacket?" she said. She started to take it off.

"I don't want it, it's ugly."

"Are you sure? It's freezing in there."

"Ma, okay, it's about to start."

My mother, my aunts, and I marched past the other mourners like we were getting our diplomas. All eyes pitied me, the only child. Well, I pitied them—the couples inching their minivans through frozen streets, the husbands grim at the wheel, the wives gym-thin and pissed, with a casserole sliding around in the backseat. The same guests would probably watch me walk down the aisle at my wedding, except they would be transformed, yarmulkes white instead of black, wrinkles powdered over, earrings stretching earlobes scrotal, lipstick that they would reapply publicly and often—whipping out compacts, holding the mirror level with their teeth.

Now my aunts were mouthing "Thank you for coming" to the guests, who were mouthing "I'm sorry" back to them. Coral mouths in motion. Hands rubbed the slack skin beneath chins. The room was a chorus of "tsk"s. I wanted to announce that my father hated it when people spoke without sound, hated the gentle clicks of tongues, the almost imperceptible suction of lips coming apart.

"Dr. Alan Jacobs was a gentle man who loved to cook," the rabbi boomed.

My aunt Sharon had bragged to the rabbi that my father had been a doctor, not realizing that the rabbi was going to use my father's full title throughout the eulogy.

"Dr. Alan Jacobs valued family and life's simple pleasures.

"Dr. Alan Jacobs worked to strengthen his community.

"Dr. Alan Jacobs was good at his work, but he knew that the real work began when he came home from the hospital.

"I never met Dr. Alan Jacobs, but I can feel his warmth in the room on this cold, snowy day."

My mother pulled tissue after tissue out of her pocketbook like a magician. She handed the damp ones to me, until I hissed, "Stop." My aunts sat with their hands clasped for Dr. Alan Jacobs, while the rabbi broke his own rule about brevity. Clearly, they all preferred the capitalized version of the man— Brother, Husband, Reader of Newspapers. But my father had undermined their efforts by refusing to leave behind solid evidence. There was no coffin at the front of the chapel, no lacquered death box with a tallis draped over it. The rabbi was lecturing about the air.

As I sat on the brown cushioned bench in Diforio Memorial, clutching my mother's soggy tissues, I started to miss college. At college, there were joints to roll and a part-time bisexual with an encyclopedic mind who came over to roll the joints and fuck. He had taken my virginity. He had memorized my mother's maiden name; he had memorized the maiden names of the mothers of the two boys he had deflowered, in addition to me. Schatz and Ducille. My mother was Tieman. Harriet Tieman, rhymes with semen.

"Are you going to tell Harriet Tieman I'm your boyfriend?" he would ask.

"You're my fake boyfriend," I said. I tried not to feel proprietary. He wasn't even in the closet. Someone had nicknamed him "Big Gay Rob." But sitting on the brown bench in Diforio Memorial, my mind wandered. Maybe the fake boyfriend was fucking someone else while I was away at my father's funeral. Maybe the fake boyfriend was fucking a boy. Without a condom.

Except, after the service, I saw him standing in the lobby with the other mourners. He was wearing a suit, and he didn't look sad enough.

"I made amazing time," he said. "Just under three hours." He named a series of highways I hadn't heard of. He handed me a sympathy card from a group of girls who lived with me. The card was actually a picture of the girls themselves, with me Photoshopped into it, and "We miss you!" scrawled over all of us.

"Are you surprised I came?" he said.

"No, I had a feeling you'd be here," I said, pretending to be psychic. I had no feeling.

LATER, AT THE SHIVA, the aunts shoved sponge cake at the fake boyfriend.

"We have too much cake," they said. "Eat it, eat it. There's too much."

They liked that he was a large man. They needed another man around, with their only brother now a box of ashes next to the stereo.

"What's your name again?" Aunt Sharon clawed his shoulder. He tried to shrug it off, but she held her grip.

"Robert," he conceded.

"Like Robert Redford." Sharon smirked like she had figured us out, then offered the fake boyfriend a macaroon.

"Aunt Shar, I didn't know you were a fan."

"Oh, I had it bad. Your father used to tease me."

Robert, unaccustomed to the chewy sweets, took a bite, then spit it into his napkin.

"We have fruit salad," Sharon said. She pivoted and sped toward melon.

"I want to meet Harriet Tieman." Robert blockaded my ear with his hand, whispered, "Not these amateurs."

Where was Harriet Tieman? She was surrounded by people reading transliterations of the Mourner's Kaddish. It was hard to see her in there, five foot nothing, holding a Xeroxed prayer.

I pushed through the throngs of fruit salad makers, fruit basket givers. One woman had brought a fruit platter inside an old Scrabble box, and everyone kept saying, "It's not Scrabble! It's not Scrabble!" Was fruit better?

"Ma, this is my friend Robert."

He stood above her, tall and blond and mostly gay, her new husband's fake boyfriend. My mother looked up, clutching a lone kiwi, Mourner's Kaddished out.

"Mrs. Jacobs, so nice to finally meet you." He shook her hand and tried to make the eye contact they'd taught him at the so-you-think-you-might-go-to-law-school orientation. She looked at his suit. It would have been too big on my father.

"Robert knows your maiden name, too," I said. "He memorized it."

"Very nice," said my mother.

How would she respond if I told her he'd put it in me? That when it was in me the third time, and no longer hurt at all, I understood everything for a second? That it could go back to its life outside me—get blow jobs in Oaxaca, intern at the ACLU—but I'd never go back to not understanding?

This maybe wasn't the right time.

"He's thinking about law school," I said.

"Don't sue us," said my mother.

Robert laughed like he was looking for a laugh. She tried to give him her kiwi. It wasn't nice, just a way for her not to be holding that fuzzy thing anymore. She told him she'd never be happy again, then offered to let him borrow my father's ties for interviews.

"Who will he give them back to?" I said.

"You."

He laughed again, declined the ties, squeezed the kiwi. Harriet Tieman was a riot. Harriet Tieman needed to lie down.

"She hates me," he said. He seemed excited.

I led him by his middle finger to one of the sofas in our living room. Now that the worst was over, everything had gotten festive. The house was snowy bright and swarming with people holding plastic cups, fizzy with ginger ale. The rabbi was in a corner by himself, eating a sandwich. The men had taken off their jackets, leaving a sun-warmed pile, and I nudged it over so Robert and I would have room to sit. I crossed my legs, then wrapped one ankle around the other calf. I wanted the rabbi to think Robert was my boyfriend.

"Where's the booze?" asked my fake boyfriend, an undergrad who had been away from home just long enough to realize that everything can be made into a joke.

"Ask the rabbi," I panned. I was also an undergrad. I had pokey nipples and there was no such thing as bisexual.

"Rabbi Irwin says we can't get drunk," said Robert, when he got back to our sofa. "It's not the custom."

"Irwin? I don't think that's his name."

But I felt drunk. I shut my eyes, leaned into some jacket scratch, slid my fist through a silky sleeve.

"Hey Robby, do you want to watch a video from when I was a kid? Do you want to watch my bat mitzvah?"

"You know that I would pay money to see that, but my French section meets at the butt crack of dawn."

"I can show you my dirty paperbacks," I said. "I think some of them were just meant to be educational about puberty."

"That sounds hot."

Robert led himself out the front door. He got into his car,

turned on the ignition, and, after waiting a few seconds for the engine to warm, backed out of my family's driveway in one smooth motion, his face already frozen into the terrible mask he wore when he thought nobody was looking.

THEN EVERYONE WAS GONE. Susan dust-busted the crumbs. She shook the tablecloth. She wedged herself between sofa legs, sucked away remains. She said, "I'm cleaning up to help your mother."

The big theme now was helping my mother. All the aunts were saying it.

"I'm staying until Wednesday to help your mother."

"I'll put coffee on to help your mother."

"It's good that you're here to help your mother."

Did reading on the couch count as helping?

Dr. Alan Jacobs loved to lie on couches and read and ignore his family sometimes. He loved to mop the floor vigorously and ask, "Could you please hang up the phone? I'm on call." But the man could be gentle. Cooking was something he liked to do.

Someone had mashed cake into the carpet and Susan plowed into it. Her legs stuck out behind her, stiff shins in poofed jeans. At some point she had changed—clamped her skirt to a hanger, flogged her jacket with a lint brush. I avoided her with a book about nocturnal emissions at tennis camp. I didn't want to watch her struggle with a suitcase zipper or sink-wash her underwear, all of the ways she kept staying.

"I wish you could stay longer, for your mother's sake," she bellowed over the buster. "But your father wouldn't want you to miss too much class."

"I'm not sure he cares anymore," I said.

She frowned. Of course he still cared. A father is a father.

She went deeper with the little vacuum, pushing her divorced torso into its vrooms, over the sofa cushions, near my legs, through the cracks. Had she ever considered a fake boyfriend? I glanced at the stereo, at the white box parked in front of it. It looked like another cake.

"Lift your feet," she said.

I WATCHED the bat mitzvah video late that night, sans Robert. If he had been in my French class in junior high, the teacher would have pronounced his name "Roh-bear." I had been, for no reason, "Rosalie."

Bonjour, Rosalie. Comment allez-vous?

Mal. Très mal. Mon père est mort.

Oui? Quel dommage!

That's all the French I could remember. Not the girl in the video. The girl in the video knew French, and, apparently, Hebrew. Enough Hebrew to bleat out a passage about cleansing your house of leprosy, after a leper has lived in your house. First, you scraped the afflicted stones. If that didn't work, you had to take the whole house apart. My parents and I met with the rabbi the week before to discuss my passage—poof, he was a rebbe and I was a scholar, not a flat-chested, staticky-haired midget. We were in the Talmud. My parents, in their work clothes, didn't seem to fit.

The rabbi stood behind a giant mahogany desk. He lit a pipe and explained that cleansing the house of disease was really a metaphor for cleansing the self of moral decay.

"That plague does sound pretty nasty," said my father, with a wink to remind anyone watching that he may have been in temple, but he loved knowing religion was irrational. He had a beeper, a teenage daughter, a wife batting pipe smoke away from her own face.

"Then someone from the Board will say a few words," said the rabbi.

"Don't be heartbroken," said my father on the drive home, "but I think we're going to quit the temple after your bat mitzvah." I had the backseat to myself and was frantically trying to memorize the opening prayers.

"It's very expensive," said my mother.

"Why am I doing this, then?"

"That rabbi is so pompous," said my father. "People kept getting sick, and someone had to tell them how to clean and quarantine so they would stop transmitting disease. It's not moral decay, it's common sense!"

My father snorted, and I sort of understood, but only enough to wish I had gotten a passage about miracles. The garage door rolled open. He dragged the garbage to the curb. She boiled water. I trudged up to my room, where I conjugated, masturbated. It wasn't hard. The young adult books were crisper then, their pages unbent, promising girls reflected in mirrors, girls with scoliosis, girls looking forward to the kind of loss that only hurt a little.

Sports Night

SPORTS NIGHT practices in the lobby. I watch them from the hall. They practice next to trophies from real sports. They practice, and detention lets out, and they are still practicing. Sports Night has no sports, only dance moves that require a thousand afterschools of practice. It's a lot of practice for one night, a lot of crying. Someone's always getting paper towels for them to cry in. I never see them be done practicing. I have to go back down the hall. I'm on Newspaper. We get out later than detention, Sports Night, Abstinence, and every real sport.

Abstinence inflates balloons for when they throw the worst party of the year. Newspaper reports on it.

"Proud virgins," we caption them.

We are ashamed virgins. We own condoms for no reason. We get As on our Sex Ed quizzes, the ones Abstinence is petitioning to get rid of. I pen an op-ed saying the school should keep the quizzes. While we're taking them, I watch girls who do Sports Night remember blow jobs they gave down by the quarry, if this town even has a quarry. I don't know where the blow jobs are. They could be anywhere.

I may not be an expert in local geography, but I do know local history. Sports Night was invented in 1948, when girls weren't allowed to play sports. Sepia-toned girls ran relay races and dodged balls in skirts past the knee. We'd beaten the Nazis. The town needed its girls to prove they could pass a baton fast enough to birth an empire. When the daughters of those girls started competing in real sports, Sports Night became more of a pageant, but kept the name that had given the town so much joy.

Sports Night has dances. It has skits. Last year's theme was Underwater Enchantment. The whole town came to see lip-synched ballads about mermaids who resented their fathers. Spandexed, bejeweled sophomores showed off months of choreography, flicked their hair around shell bras, lowered themselves into splits between legs coated with glitter. Every character was sexy. It wasn't just the mermaid. They had sexy lobsters, sexy squid. They keep one character not sexy to cover up the few fat girls who don't know they're not supposed to audition for Sports Night.

I know I'm not supposed to audition. I don't know how I know—nobody tells you you can't—but there are conflicts. Newspaper, for instance, and a club where kids without friends meet with the principal to discuss how to improve the school. Why students of different races sit separately in the cafeteria is one of our concerns, as well as Abstinence being mad that the cafeteria windows get decorated every Christmas for Hanu-Kwanzaa but we leave out the infant Jesus. Sports Night gets a window, too. They stand on cafeteria chairs in leggings they don't mind getting paint on, and reveal their theme the first Monday of every December.

This year's theme is the decade when their moms were pretty. The costume is easy if the mom kept her clothes, if she was the same size as the girl. My mom was pretty, too, then, but I'm not pretty this decade. I thought about doing a skit about it, a dance. One of the colleges I'm applying to lets you do dances about your mom for credit. It lets you do dances about the girls who did dances in your high school. That's why I'm watching them. I'm going to need their moves later, when I'm taking Interpretative Dance II with people like me.

SOMEBODY set off the smoke alarm and now all the clubs are waiting on the field behind the school—Chess, Newspaper, Suicide Awareness. Sports Night keeps practicing. They lunge, clutch grass. Editors nudge me, as if I made this happen. The editors look worse outside. At Newspaper, they're in charge, ordering pizza, editing last year's Band trip article to fit this year's Band trip needs. Out here, they're just a group of kids who brought their backpacks in case there was really a fire.

Chess brought their chess sets with them. During a smoke alarm last May, somebody moved a rook and disrupted a championship game. Now they bring the sets outside, balance them like pizzas while they wait on the grass. I'm impressed by Chess, the interracial makeup of its nerds. I like their little timers.

"Should we do an article about Chess?" I ask a Josh with a backpack. The Josh's backpack has his initials on it—JAG—so he doesn't get mistaken for any of the other nerds of his race. "They seem ignored."

"Chess doesn't want not to be ignored," he says.

Textbook corners frame his initials from inside his backpack. He carries all his textbooks with him at all times, like he was never assigned a locker. I have the same textbooks—AP Physics, AP American, AP Foreign-Language-Not-Spoken-Since-Ancient-Times.

"We did a double issue for Sports Night," I say. "We had pictures of all those lobsters. You interviewed Lindsay."

"She was a captain," he says.

"Well, she's a captain again, but I'm not interviewing her," I say. Sports Night is doing rib isolations. "Fuck it, I'm interviewing Chess."

"We can't put pawns on the front page!" he yells after me.

"Can we put suicide?"

JAG's the reason I'm not editor in chief this year. Around the time of last year's Band trip, he and I interviewed for the same job. He wore a tie. I found my evaluation sheet after, and it said, "Leaves the pub shop during production and we don't know where she goes." I could have told them if they had asked. I break into the Abstinence office and spray it with contraceptive foam. I practice Sports Night moves in an empty classroom. I watch the sun set out a suicide-proof window and remain firmly inside what's supposed to be my life.

MY MOM picked me up the night I found out I didn't get chief. I was crying. I would have to be on Newspaper another year, taking orders from someone my own age with a giant backpack.

"Did you put the paper to bed?" she asked. She liked to picture me tucking the newspaper in.

"They can burn in hell," I said.

"Just being on the masthead of a respected weekly is enough, Li," she said. "You can still put *Argus* on your applications without the headache of being in charge."

"I would have taken the paper in a new direction," I said.

"Maybe people like the old direction," she said. "Why don't you drive home?"

Her offer let me know she was sorry. My driving skills were not getting me into college. I had crept up many curbs practicing my K turns, had gone down one-way streets in a new direction. My parents took turns not taking me out.

Now I drive fine. Not everyone on Newspaper can say the same. Some of their moms still pick them up on Production Night, though they hold the title of chief.

"LINDSAY," I ask Lindsay, with Newspaper's tape recorder, "how are you deciding team costumes this year in the absence of clear characters like enchanted fish and turtles?"

"We have characters," she says. "From that decade."

"You mean famous people? Like Valerie Solanas?"

"We're not doing her," says Lindsay. "Mrs. Spumondi says it has to be inclusive for everyone. The whole town comes."

"Yes, the whole town came last year. Male attendance was especially high. How did you feel about your friends' fathers and the guy from the post office seeing you in those sexy lobster costumes?" This is my hardball.

"We're proud of our bodies," she says.

I hadn't thought of that, but Lindsay is well versed in defending Sports Night from a short-lived club that formed in opposition to Sports Night. Nobody remembers them now. Abstinence came and stole their thunder by being opposed to sex overall.

"Okay, Lindsay. Thank you for your time."

"Thanks for watching us practice." She smiles at me like I'm one of the male teachers who also watches them practice.

"I need to watch for the article."

The truth is that I'm not sure I would have passed Driver's Ed last year if Mr. Hinkle and I hadn't spent so much time together watching Sports Night practice in the lobby.

"No DUI fatalities this weekend," I'd say, disappointed. You needed to hand in thirty DUI fatalities from local newspapers in order to pass the class.

"How do they kick so high?" he'd wonder.

"Maybe I'm not looking in the right papers."

"Someone will drink and drive soon," promised Hinkle. "Birds gotta swim. Are you thinking of trying out for this?"

I kicked to show him that my heel hardly cleared the floor, forcing the reluctant, throat-driven laugh of a man who must occasionally use an emergency brake. Mrs. Spumondi told us we were free to leave if we didn't respect the practice. Mrs. Spumondi's not a teacher or anybody's mother. She's old. She just runs Sports Night. She may have invented Sports Night.

She at least kept it going, long after we had girls dribbling balls, swinging bats, and kicking something other than the air. Now Mrs. Spumondi delegates. She selects the teacher-judges, assigns formerly hot moms to a committee that decides if the basketball hoop is a decent place to hang balloons.

Newspaper wants me to find out what else the mom committee does, but I tell the editors I'm busy with suicide now. I'm quitting Newspaper. They don't know yet, but my article on Suicide Awareness will be my last—in effect, my suicide note. I've realized I don't like reporting on the school.

The school shouldn't blame itself. It's just a school, the kind that bans glue sticks and hats. I'm tired of having opinions about the bans. I never sniffed a glue stick. I never wore a hat. I tried to sniff a glue stick once and nothing happened. Maybe you need to eat them.

Also, the acceptance letters from colleges should be here

any day now, the decal for my mother's car. So she doesn't get mistaken for the other moms of her race.

THIS YEAR Hinkle acts like he doesn't know me anymore. Kids come out of detention, hug him, go back in detention. He's kind of their mascot. It has to do with that the kids who get detention are also the best drivers. I've ridden in the backs of the Ed cars when they're at the helm, and the ride is smooth. Hinkle never uses the brake with them, never says, "Pull over immediately, or I will have no choice but to use the emergency brake." They hand in fifteen fatalities, and he's fine with it. He lets them smoke in the cars.

Sports Night girls take smoke breaks. They crouch in their leggings on the concrete steps, stretch their hamstrings, gossip, cry.

I go out there and find Lindsay in tears.

"What's the problem?"

"People are abusing their power." She lights a cigarette with one of her old bat mitzvah matches.

"I thought you were a captain," I say.

"Who are you again?"

"I interviewed you for *The Argus*."

"That Josh guy interviewed me, too," she says, coughs.

"When?"

"He said he needed to ask me some stuff you'd forgotten."

"He always does this. He undermines my relationships with my sources. I'm quitting."

"I'm quitting, too."

I don't know what she's quitting, smoking or her dance team, but it doesn't matter. We sit on the steps and quit for a while. Lindsay's matches say "I shopped till I dropped at Lindsay's Bat!" Her bat mitzvah theme was shopping. Guests were assigned to sit at tables labeled Bloomingdale's, the mall, the Gap. Everyone got a little credit card with their name on it. I wasn't invited, but I remember teachers confiscating the Lindsay cards at school, as though they paid for things in a junior high black market.

"I hate Sports Night," she says. "At this point, I actually hate it."

"We could switch places," I say. I picture myself ablaze with blush in the gym on Sports Night, cat-crawling across the volleyball court, telling a reporter I'm just proud of my body.

"So I would have to be on the school newspaper? Nobody reads that."

"That's not why we do it. We do it for college."

"That's not why you do it," she says. Before I can find out why I do it, detention comes out of the building and turns the steps into a skateboard ramp, a dangerous, bumpy thing.

MY MOM won't let me quit. She says we're not a family of quitters. She shows me her yearbook to prove she was on committees. A committee to plant flowers, a committee to end the war.

"Didn't you basically want the U.S. to quit the war?" I say. "Quitting is powerful."

"*The Argus* is not a war," she says.

"They both exploit the young," I say.

"You sound like Alan," she says. I'm not sure if my father is antiwar or anti-*Argus*. He works late and my mom likes to turn me into him when he's not home. When he is home, my parents talk about things I'm not interested in, like homeowners' insurance, or how much it will cost to fix the scratch I put on the car. They have no extracurriculars anymore. It's hard for them to see what they could give to this town.

WHEN SPORTS NIGHT arrives, it's Lindsay I follow. I follow her through several songs gay men used to dance to before the virus, and a skit about the yo-yo. I take notes for Newspaper. They're not just doing dances from that time. They're doing dances from now: pops and locks, the Dougie, the Butterfly. They lip-synch their songs. They lip-synch their skits. Spumondi takes notes on a clipboard. It's unclear what decade we're in.

Balloons hang all around. Boys pop them with pencils, get threatened with detention.

"But it's Saturday," a popper argues. "You can't get detention on Saturday."

He's right. We're in the school, but we're not in school. The bans don't apply Saturday. Kids wear hats. Teachers wear jeans. Kids run around saying, "Mr. Hinkle's wearing jeans." JAG doesn't have his backpack on and looks like a dismembered turtle. He looks good.

"Make sure to write down the order of the dances," he says.

"You're micromanaging me, Josh."

JAG's notebooks all say Joshua Aaron Geller in block letters on the front.

"In your suicide article," he says, "you left out the name of the girl who committed suicide."

"I thought we had to protect her privacy. You know, she did Sports Night last year? But they made her be a swordfish."

"Fact-check that," says Josh.

A group of boys starts throwing pencils at us, or maybe we're just in the way of what they're aiming at. Josh picks up a pencil gently, like it's a gift.

"I wonder who's going to be traumatized this year," he says.

I think about Lindsay on the steps, but Lindsay's not crying now. She's smiling through her eye shadow, inexplicably dressed as a French maid, crawling across the floor near a pile of balloons. We're both traitors to quitting. I got my college acceptance letters last week, but I'm still here, reporting from a laminated bleacher on a Saturday. The guy from the post office is here, too. He comes every year.

Lindsay straddles her feather duster. I still can't figure out how this costume fits into the theme. Maybe there's a sitcom about a maid from that decade? Or maybe she's the housewife on the show where the witchy wife controls her husband with her appliances? She twitches her nose at a girl dressed as an ad executive. Boys from the school start chanting, "Ride that broom! Ride that broom!" and soon men from the town join in.

"This theme is disturbing," says Josh.

"She's just confident in her sexuality," I say.

He eyes me like he can't believe I made the honor roll.

"No, really," I say. "What are we doing that's so much more important than what she's doing?"

"I don't know," he says. "Preparing for our futures?"

"Our bright futures in journalism?" I say. I fight with boys instead of dancing for them. "Are we going to be Woodward and Bernstein? You said in Debate practice that you wanted to be a prosecutor."

This isn't fair. We lie in applications. We lie in interviews. We lie everywhere but on top of each other. The town's men are screaming around Josh, a boy who became a man by memorizing United States currency fluctuations in the decades before girls were allowed to play sports. Josh sits up straighter, unable to look at Lindsay on the floor now, like if he studies her any longer he will memorize her. He will turn into something else.

"It's all good practice," he says. "You know that."

But they practice, too. It's paid off. The whole thing looks like a never-ending halftime show, a sluttier version of a tumultuous time. The next dance number is even sexier than Lindsay's, but the team burns a bra during their skit and gets disqualified for creating a fire hazard. Now girls I haven't interviewed are crying. Their captain tells Spumondi to go fuck herself. Parents around me take sides, with some pledging allegiance to their daughters' teams, and some saying Sports Night has gotten out of control.

The principal runs down the bleacher steps and announces that Sports Night is canceled. Every girl on the floor starts crying. People boo. I'm taking notes. The teachers turn into teachers again and start telling everyone they have to go home.

"See you Monday!" they say, as though we have a choice.

"See you Monday!" says Josh. He takes his cues from those in power.

"Wait, I think we have our headline," I say. For once, I'm breaking new news. "Sports Nights Celebrates Past, but Future Hangs in the Balance."

"What future?" he says.

"Its future. The event's future."

"Yes!" he says. We slap five, the kiss of nerds. "This is going to be a great issue."

Communication Arts

Dear Student A,

I'm sorry I put a sentence from your recent essay up on
the SmartBoard without explaining to the rest of the class
that they were critiquing writing by a fellow classmate. It
was not smart of me, no matter what the board is called.
I'm sorry that Student B said that his advice for how to fix
your sentence was "Start over." He believed that we were
critiquing work by an anonymous student writer, perhaps
from another college altogether. As you correctly pointed out
during class, his advice was "too harsh." I agree that criticism
should be constructive. At the same time, I did not want to
say that his advice was wrong. Sometimes the best thing
we can do in writing is start over. Still, I am sorry you felt
humiliated in front of the class. I know English is not your
first language. You told me that if you could write an essay

in Russian, you would not make as many mistakes as you are making in English. Please know that I find it impressive that you wrote a complex and thoughtful essay on "Daddy" by Sylvia Plath. I could not do the same in Russian if I had only lived in Russia for two years! Student B didn't mean to offend, I'm sure.

Best,

Professor S

Dear Student B,

I'm sorry I didn't explain that we were critiquing your classmate's work before putting Student A's work on the board. I know you felt bad about your comment, but it is my responsibility as the teacher to warn students in advance if you will be giving feedback to people who are physically in the room.

As for your grade, that remains to be seen. I'd like you to come to class more than once every three weeks. You write well, and you challenged the idea that toddler playpens are more humane than child leashes, which showed a willingness to take risks with ideas, even though the children-on-leashes discussion strayed too far from the poem we were discussing. Why are you at community college? You could go to a four-year college if you worked a little harder.

All the best,

Professor S

Dear Student B,

Regarding my last email, I didn't mean to imply that a four-year college is necessarily better than a two-year college.

College is dumb, jobs are few. All of you are becoming nutritionists or nurses or physical therapists and will probably make more money than I do adjuncting at your community college. I make enough to pay rent, but not to afford all of the dresses I wear to class. My creditors are going to come get me one of these days. By creditors, I mean credit cards. They have booths in front of the school to trick you into going into debt early. They sure tricked me, with my master's in English Literature and my thesis on the advertisements in English periodicals where serial novels first appeared. What did those ads say about Victorian society? What were they trying to trick women into trying?

Do you study child development or marine biology? Though our class is in the Marine Building, I have yet to meet a student who studies marine life. Most of the Marine Building is for the Fashion Department. They are looking for models. I saw a sign. Perhaps the Russian girl you inadvertently insulted in class could apply. She's tall and wears clothes well.

Sincerely,
Professor S

Hi Student C,

I am sorry you weren't feeling well enough to come to class today. Morning sickness can be tough. Some of my friends have experienced it. I have not, though I am twelve years older than you. My mother keeps sending me articles about Oocyte Cryopreservation, but I worry about the defrosting process. Can that be safe? Plus, being a single mother looks like no picnic. Will you be going it alone?

Please bring a printed copy of your essay to our next class to avoid further penalties for lateness.

Best,

Professor S

Student A,

Thank you. Or спасибо, as they say in Russian. You guys have some great writers. It's a shame that we had to read *The Cherry Orchard* in translation. I'm glad that things are smoothed out between you and Student B. He is a young man and sometimes doesn't think before he speaks, though he is majoring in Communication Arts, a major I don't totally understand, except that it means he is required to take more English classes. What are you studying?

Prof S

Dear Student F,

If you do not turn in your paper by the next class meeting, you will get an F on the paper and it will be difficult for you to pass the course. I gave you an extension after your grandmother died, but a month has passed since then. Unless your grandmother raised you, or played a central role during your childhood, grandparent grief is not the kind of grief that makes essay writing impossible. The death of a grandparent in college is a natural occurrence and happens to at least one student per semester, usually when an essay is due.

If you continue to have trouble processing your loss, there are support groups on campus. I am sending you a link. Please bring your essay to the next class to avoid further penalties for lateness.

All best,
Professor S

Dear Student B,

You and Student A seem to be getting along well these days. I am pleased when students in my class become friends. At the same time, I would like you to remain respectful while other students are speaking and not carry on side conversations during class discussions. Student A is quite fetching, with her blond hair and her Russian accent, but it is crucial to your participation grade that you stay focused on the class discussion, even if you find the story "obvious" or "moralistic." To be honest, I have never liked Hawthorne, either. He goes on the syllabus for the symbolism unit and so I feel like I have covered my bases re: 19th Century American literature, but I think I will replace him next year with Melville.

We can reschedule your appointment for Tuesday. If you're going to miss that meeting as well, please text me instead of emailing me.

Best,
Professor S

Dear Student D,

I'm so sorry to hear about your legal troubles. Please look online to find the appropriate forms for withdrawing from my class.

Professor S

Dear Student E,

You're right. I should not have yelled at you or slammed my fist down on the SmartBoard control panel. I was frustrated that you and Student M were laughing at Student Q, whose learning difficulties are obvious to all. You are not in high school anymore. But it was wrong of me to respond to immaturity with unmitigated rage. Two wrongs do not make a right, and I would like to model better behavior for you and Student M, who often enter class late holding iced mocha drinks. These drinks leave small puddles on the desks. While the desks are Formica and the marks do not cause permanent damage, the puddles can wet the handouts or the SmartBoard stylus should I rest these items on the desks upon which you have rested the iced mocha drinks.

Have you considered making an appointment with Psych Services? Therapy can be beneficial, even to bullies. Especially to bullies. Power is what you are enjoying, though I've noticed a look on your face sometimes that suggests you don't feel powerful at all. Student M has no idea what she feels. Being a teacher offers the temptation to abuse one's power, but I find that firmness and kindness are usually effective enough to manage a classroom, even a classroom full of adults who behave as though they're in the throes of puberty.

You're currently averaging a B– in the class, but could manage a B if you focus your attentions on the upcoming final and come to the rest of the class meetings *on time.*

Sincerely,
Professor S

Student A,

I'm sorry you feel that way. Of course I am happy that you and Student B found love this semester. I'd like to think that some of the literature we read deepened the connection you made to each other. Seating you separately was a decision I made because you two could not stop whispering during class. I know you think you are speaking softly, but even whispers can be distracting. You've spent the last few classes punishing me for this decision, snickering at my lectures and occasionally suggesting that I "start over." Please reconsider your behavior. We're rounding the corner to June. Let's finish the year on a high note!

Thanks,
Professor S

Dear Dean Z,

The reports you've gotten about my conduct are understandably disturbing, but I believe that the "evidence" against me has been misconstrued. I never had intimate contact with Student B. Halfway through the semester, Student A and Student B began dating. Student A was jealous that Student B would sometimes ask me along on their movie dates. I always refused. I have no interest in going to the multiplex to see the latest Caucasian stoner heist with a couple of nineteen-year-olds. I never spend time with my students outside of school grounds, save the occasional shuttle bus ride to or from campus, where we have no choice but to chat. The shuttle bus is invaluable for those of us on the faculty without cars. On the bus, I keep the talk on neutral subjects such as the weather and the requirements of the course.

Yes, Student B had my phone number. He had neglected to email me about canceling a prior meeting, so I decided that texts would be a more efficient way for him to reach me. The texts where I say that he is an adult with the right to make his own decisions were not about a decision to be with me, but rather about his decision to quit school. Student B is very intelligent, but he has not completed any assignments, and seems stifled by the many graduation requirements of our institution. I never encouraged him to drop out. I merely suggested that college might not be the best use of his or his family's financial resources if he fails the same English course every semester. Student B is a talented musician, but neither his family nor his girlfriend support him in this endeavor. As educators, we're supposed to value school above all else, but we must remember that a college learning environment is not for everyone. Again, I am sorry that I got involved in a matter that should have remained between the student, his parents, and his academic adviser. Student A forwarded my texts to you either because she misunderstood them (English is not her first language) or because she wanted to cause me harm.

As for the more explicit texts, I find them as shocking as you do. I hope that the spelling errors and the use of sex message slang indicate that they are the work of someone younger. I don't even know what many of those abbreviations mean.

If you'd like to discuss this matter further, I am available early next week. I take my job as an adjunct professor of English very seriously, and hope that we can clear up any remaining confusion. Coffee?

Sincerely,
Professor S

Dear Student G,

Thank you for the rose. I hope you didn't pick it on campus.

Best,

Professor S

Little Girl

SHE SLEPT WITH MEN who only wanted to play *Settlers of Catan*. She slept with law students who had framed copies of the Constitution on their bedroom walls. She slept with sound architects, sound engineers, and the second baseman from her softball league. She hardly ever slept. Sometimes she took a pill, but often she lay awake next to a sleeping man, trying to read the Bill of Rights in the dark, then called a taxi and went home. She liked riding in the back of a taxi at night. It felt private, even with the driver up front. She liked recognizing the streets closer to her building, and she liked the deli where she sometimes went to get money to pay the driver. She'd grab a can of condensed milk, a hairnet. She wasn't sure what for.

The men never called. They sent her smiley-face permutations and pictures of their cocks, but not one had called her since the year 2004. That man had met her at a flash mob in a department store, then looked her up in the last phone book the phone company ever printed. She had lived in a different building then, had withdrawn cash at a different deli, and needed a landline to communicate with parents who didn't trust cell phones yet. She and the man dated for five months, but things never got as good as figuring out that he had found her in the phone book.

She slept with men who were sober for no reason. She found this more alarming than if they had once been alcoholics. She slept with recovering alcoholics, suffering workaholics, and a heroin addict who wanted them to have the same spirit animal. The heroin addict was writing a memoir about overcoming heroin addiction. Having a deadline for his memoir had stressed him out so much that he had started using heroin again.

Some of the men carried condoms in their wallets, like it was the fifties. It was not the fifties. One day, it would be the 2050s, and she would have to do this all over again in a retirement community. In between, she'd get married, get widowed. She'd miss him, but would be grateful for all the years they'd had together. Where was she going to meet her future late husband? At work? At work, she'd met an anthropology professor by the copy machines who called her "little girl" in bed. She was thirty-two. But he was even older. He didn't like what she had been photocopying, a text by a continental theorist whose opinion of history most straight men considered misinformed. Her students handed in papers about the theorist's work that began, "This story confused me at first." She didn't sleep with her students. They were too confused.

She slept with a man who didn't keep any food in his house. He was a used-book dealer, and there were piles of signed first editions in his oven. Another used-book dealer had hair on the shaft of his penis and a panic attack in her bedroom. Used-book dealers, she decided, were the worst. She liked books, but she didn't care about the edition. New things were okay with her. Everything got old soon enough anyway.

She slept with younger men. She didn't really have a choice. Men her own age were busy going bald, acquiring bald offspring. Men her own age had jobs like "head of school," "program facilitator," and "lawyer." She tried to be excited that the men she slept with were younger, but she was just as excited if they were older, or the same age. Her body acted the same no matter who touched her. It had been that way since college, when she'd slept with a man who didn't take his sweater off during the act. She'd found it a nice break from skin. He had later transferred. Some of the men she slept with had studied abroad, some had taken time off, but all of them had gone. Her body valued education.

Her body valued her body. She took long showers, ate avocados, stretched while chanting in Sanskrit, and slept her way through the phone book. There was no more phone book, but she had names in her phone, first names only: Davids and Adams, Lukes, Sams. She'd get a message at night—*What are you doing right now?*—and go. What was she doing? Sometimes she didn't know exactly who was messaging her and it would be a surprise when she got there: which David, which Sam. Some of the buildings had elevators and she enjoyed the anticipation on the ride up, the soreness on the ride down. What happened in between almost didn't happen. She'd wind up back where she started, walk into the street, and hail a cab.

Schwartz, Spiegel, Zaveri, Cho

THERE WERE WAYS to touch Schwartz wrong.

If I pulled too hard, he would say, "Ow! Are you trying to pull my dick off?"

Everyone would agree that was wrong. Schwartz's dick should not be pulled off.

If I pulled too soft, Schwartz would say nothing, maybe even lose the hardness, and the softness would be my fault. Then Schwartz would say, "Never mind," and Spiegel would tell him, "Never trust a girl to do what you can do better yourself."

So why bring us in? To do what you can do, worse?

The place to do it worse was here, in the absence of parents, at Geology Camp. Last year, I had gone to Space. The year before that, International Relations. The nerds stayed the same. In the sunny summer sun, they took measurements, reenacted diplomacy. I was small and eager, though I often forged my data.

Some days I skipped Topography, claimed menstrual head-
aches, took puberty-enhancing naps. I was working toward a
certificate in Stratification, which meant you got to handle plastic models of rocks not native to the area, but I had learned
you could make yourself invisible to a science teacher making
summer money by simply not showing up at the allotted time.
After a while, they stopped calling your name, assumed you'd
gone home.

There was no science at home, but there were also no boys.
I wasn't about to call my parents from Geology Camp's one pay
phone and demand they come get me. They believed that I was
learning and that all learning mattered. It didn't matter that
the moon at Space Camp wasn't the moon. On the night of our
lunar mission, we lay in sleeping bags on a tennis court, ate
dehydrated ice cream, walked around in slow motion. The real
moon we ignored, or justified as the moon of a distant planet.

The oldest boys with the deepest acne wore the T-shirts of
the colleges they planned to be accepted to. They called each
other by last names only—Schwartz, Spiegel, Zaveri, Cho. They
studied maps like we were actually going somewhere. They
made jokes about cleavage, where rocks break apart. They made
jokes about hardness, their own, calcite's. It was unclear what
any of them had touched or been touched by. Cho often spoke
of "girls from home." A possibility existed that there were girls
from home whose reputations were so besmirched that they
were willing to service a member of the National Honor Society,
but I couldn't imagine Cho unzipping for one. We all aspired
to orgasm, but were afraid of our GPAs slipping.

Everything counted. We aced Sex Ed. We took up the clari-
net, got too good for regular band, and hung out with the
band teacher in a special class devoted to jazz. Spiegel brought
his trombone to camp, Zaveri his tenor sax. I spent rest hour

practicing my trumpet. The two of them could play backup. We'd call it an independent project, rack up extra credit at our respective schools.

Yet I wasn't sure a camp counted. This was the beginning of a crack between where I then stood and where I would one day kneel. Most of these boys ruined their legs with the wrong sneakers and ankle-gripping socks, but through their basketball shorts I caught an outline of what I could learn. The edge of a Cornell tee brushed against a new pectoral. I liked the way Schwartz said "Feldspar" and the way he held a graphing calculator. It had weight in his hands.

"Can I borrow your calculator, Schwartz?"

He looked confused, then annoyed. Didn't I have my own calculator? The calculators cost more than we had ever spent on a school supply.

"I lost it and I'm scared to tell my parents."

Schwartz rolled his eyes. He wasn't scared of his parents. I shrugged (I was scared of mine), then poked his calf. That seemed low enough on his leg that he could mistake it for a mistake.

"I need this," he said, catching on, poke-wise. "But there's an extra in my cabin."

"During evening activity," I said, "they don't take attendance."

Schwartz took me to his cabin while everyone else was applauding the visiting fossil expert. The cabin smelled like incense, socks, spunk, the woods. Schwartz showed me a *Playboy.* He was showing himself the *Playboy,* but I needed to be a witness. The *Playboy* didn't come with instructions for what to do with Schwartz after it was done with its job. Schwartz presumably knew.

"Is this alright?" said Schwartz, reaching up my shirt.

"Is this alright?" said Schwartz, reaching up my shorts.

I wasn't sure why you were supposed to stop them. I wasn't sure why you had to call them by their last names. It had to do with too many of their first names being the same name.

Schwartz did a couple of things wrong and then it was my turn. I wanted to ask about the skin. Did you pull the skin along the core of hardness, like a sleeve, or did you grab skin and core together as one?

My hand stayed in place. I didn't ask Schwartz "How?" I wanted to already know. I didn't want Spiegel to tell Schwartz that Schwartz could have done it better himself. Let Spiegel do it better himself, was my feeling. Schwartz had brought me here.

Schwartz put his hand over my hand, and started to move the pair of us. It wasn't rocket science, or even rock science. It wasn't an earthquake, but something began to move in me. Every test we studied for was nothing. This was the kind of test where they see if babies can breathe. Most of them can.

"David," I said, "you can let go."

The hand job worked. I didn't own any lube then, though we could have used the lotion under Schwartz's cot. I didn't use his lotion, or saliva from my tongue, but soon my hand was wet with the infinite possibilities inside Schwartz.

He wiped my fist with a roll of toilet paper he had stolen from the bathroom. There it sat, above his bed, in case he caught a summer cold, or for nights when he had to do it better himself.

"The calculator," he said. "I can't find an extra. You're not going to be able to do well without one."

"This camp doesn't count," I said.

"Who told you that?" His shorts were back on his body, his feet huge in flip-flops. One day you were children together, the next day the boys had giant feet. Tomorrow Schwartz would be hunched over a magnifying glass, identifying crystal formations in closed-toe shoes.

"We just come here to show that we're curious," I said. "Nobody cares if we actually are. And I have a calculator."

"You're not like anyone in New Jersey," he said.

I doubted this was true. Somewhere in Teaneck, in Fair Lawn, a girl like me was learning to stroke the college bound.

"You've never had a girl do what I did?"

"I lost my virginity at Oceanography Camp," he said. "But not much has happened since then."

"You're not a virgin? Does Spiegel know?"

"Spiegel doesn't know anything," he said.

What We Bought

HE BOUGHT ME FLOWERS and a vase. He gave me the vase three days after he gave me the flowers. I don't know what he thought would happen in the interim, maybe that I would just leave the flowers on the table, and the flowers would die there. He wrote, "Don't forget to trim the stems!" so I guess he thought I would put the flowers in something, like a jar, which I did do, but the jar was not tall enough for the flowers, even after I trimmed the stems, so I had to go out and buy my own vase.

I bought the vase at a complicated store that also sold chrysanthemums and soap. The woman who owned the store tried to show me a vase that cost more than a hundred dollars, a heavy vase with flowers embossed on the glass. For a minute, I thought I needed a vase that cost more than a hundred dollars. Then I asked the woman if she had anything else. She started removing flowers from a cheaper vase. Maybe she had never sold a vase before.

By the time I got the vase from him, I already had a vase. It only cost twelve dollars. I don't know how much his vase cost, but somewhere between twelve and a hundred. I'm going to guess forty. Later, I gave the vase he bought me to my aunt.

"This will look good in your dining room," I told her. "Take it. I can't look at it anymore."

My aunt loved that I couldn't look at a vase a man had given me. Giving her my vase made it seem like gifts from men happened to me all the time, or at least often enough that I would know what to do with one. I had gotten other gifts from other men: a parasol, a record, a box of tea. Those times, I had set the gifts down in the vestibule of my building until someone took them away. The parasol and the record went fast. The tea nobody would take. I watched it sit in the vestibule, next to the mailboxes, day after day. Finally, I brought the tea back upstairs to my apartment and threw it in the garbage.

My aunt told her dinner guests the story of the vase the night she got it, then told the story again a few more times before the vase and the story of the vase stopped being new to her.

Tips

THE COMFORT INN was across the street. But we were sleeping by the side of the road. The back of Mindal's car folded out into a bed, and parked in front of her car was a motor home, where Charley, our pimp, slept. He wasn't a pimp in the traditional sense. He jerked off in front of a computer for money, and tonight we would join him, for more money, all to fund the decals for her car, the greens for our salads. "Camming for kale" was what we called it when we were clever, punning, hungry. Our tastes tended expensive. Mindal spoke of dumpster diving, but she never dove. She was still a girl from a gourmet suburb, same as me. We'd had homeroom together, drawn ovaries on each other's binders. We'd refused to stand for the Pledge of Allegiance, first to protest some invasion, and then, when the invasion had ended, more quickly than we'd expected, to protest the ongoing covert operations we knew were ongoing. Mindal's mom got that radio station, the one where radical nutritionists had their own shows, told you to stop eating everything and get vitamin infusions. Once a month, Mindal's parents took her to the city for an infusion.

"I feel terrific!" she'd say, a fourteen-year-old high on taurine and St. John's Wort. "I feel alive."

Now she needed to not have a job to feel alive, to have skin burnt because sunblock was full of carcinogens, and I wanted some of this life for myself, though I carried a mini sunblock in my purse and applied it whenever she went to pee in gas stations. I was less scared of the cam, though, had more groove when it came to unprofessional porn, which I had enjoyed on and off, as a consumer, for years.

Charley was from somewhere north—difficult weather—mudslides, earthquakes, tornado warnings. He was sick of the moss. He was taking donations from anyone who wanted to see him naked in front of a tie-dyed sheet.

"Tips," he called both the money and the men who gave the money.

"Whatever you ladies are comfortable doing," he'd told us. "Tips will tip."

"We're comfortable making you dinner," said Mindal, chopping greens. I was on garlic detail. The motor home was homey, had beaded curtains, a spice rack.

"Your place looks nice," I said. I worried about Charley sometimes. He was a bunch younger than us. He referred to women as ladies.

"It was my mom's ride," he said. "She sold it to me."

"Does she know about Charleycumsalot?"

"She thinks it's funny. My son the porn star."

My daughter the porn star struck me as something that neither Mindal's nor my mom would find funny, no matter what radio station they listened to. So far we had just licked his cheeks while wearing American flag bikini tops, played the part of cam bitches in the motor home.

"We're not on spring break," Charley clarified for those watching at home, the working stiffs with wi-fi. "This is our lifestyle."

"8inchinUtah wants to know: Have you two ever made out?"

"Can't best friends just be best friends anymore?" asked Mindal.

Best friends couldn't be best friends and earn anything from Utah. Back in her car, we debated if we could kiss each other on the lips, no tongue. She needed waterproof pants and a special kind of rope. Rock climbing was another reason not to have a normal job. The climbers worked on oil rigs, trimmed weed, sold afghans, or, if they were really good, got sponsored by their own equipment. Most of them were men, or the girl-friends of men, but Mindal wanted to subvert the paradigm, or at least become a girlfriend. In the meantime, she got Charley to lend us his gear.

Mindal led the pitches and I followed. I didn't want the rope to break, or even stretch.

"It has to stretch a little," she said.

She tried to explain how different types of rope worked, the advantages and disadvantages of her ATC, the money she was saving for a van, but I started zoning out when talk turned to her van. I turned it back to kissing.

"We can pretend we don't know each other."

"We're cuter than most of the girls on the site."

"Girls next door. He can say he met us next door."

Mindal had met Charley at a crag, while I was still pulling plastic at Indoor Boulders and thinking I was going up. This was when I got vertical on the wall without the weed, trickier than it sounds, like bowling with a heavier ball. Sport of the mind. Charley's sister grew medicinal strains up north, but Charley had decided to be the sober child of addicts, so Mindal and I passed a joint in her car.

"He's pretty judgy about drugs," I said.

"He lets us use his bathroom. And his stove. He builds perfect anchors."

"But we buy all the food."

"It's just until we make enough to climb without him. Let's just fucking kiss, okay? We know we're not gay. Who cares what the internet thinks?"

"I could go back to the law office."

"The real estate guy? He evicts people for money. Marx says landlords are the scum of the earth."

"Get the *Manifesto*. I want to see where he says that."

"It's in *Das Kapital*," she said. "Rent is bullshit."

Owning a van was not bullshit. Nobody could evict you from a van, though they could snatch it if you went bankrupt. A van could break down. There was more to understand about vans than I was prepared to learn. I could type quickly and edit Charleycumsalot's About Me ("I am a 19-year-old male who luvs loves trad climbing and pleasuring himself"). I could proofread the van repair manual, but I could not repair. Sex work required a willingness I thought I might have if I didn't have parents. My mother watched one hour of television a week. She gave hugs freely and wasn't addicted to anything except Tylenol.

"This is a class issue," I said.

"Just because his parents were coke dealers doesn't make him a different class. Coke is expensive."

"His father went to jail. Your father is an accountant."

"It's a fine line. Don't you want to get out of society? We hate society. We've always hated it, ever since that idiot homeroom teacher made us turn our Pro-Choice T-shirts inside out."

"We shouldn't have listened. We had the First Amendment on our side."

"That's one of the only decent laws," she admitted. She buried the roach in a mint tin. "But it doesn't matter. The law is worthless. We have to leave society."

"We're still in society." I looked across the street. The hotel pool shimmered. Maybe we could sleep in the hotel. My mother would pay. I'd tell her it was an emergency, that we had almost been sex trafficked. In the morning, Mindal could drive me back to the city, where I would resume typing 3-Day Notices to irresponsible tenants. The lawyer didn't require loyalty, only a willingness to never stop typing. He and I had the same birthday. It created a bond that allowed me to quit for weeks at a time as long I continued to forward him our shared horoscope.

"The risks you take today will reap great rewards."

For him that probably meant trying a new Turkish restaurant. For me it meant showing my nipples to agoraphobes who preferred watching tit in real time. I put on my American flag bikini top. We had found the bikinis in a thrift store on our drive north from the Bay. Mindal wore hers with a matching flag bandanna when we went grocery shopping, endured catcalls in wine country telling her it wasn't 1969. Dumber oenophiles thought her patriotic.

She took off her shirt and opened the car door.

"Where's your bikini?" I said. I had counted on her being scared of the cam so I could be the one to say it was okay to be scared.

"I'm going topless tonight," she said. "We need to make some money."

We'd make porn, not war. There were new wars, a lot like

the old wars. Charley was the right age to enlist. If Mindal fucked him, did I get to keep any of the money? What could I do on camera, stand there explaining local rent regulations, how to outsmart your landlord? Braid Mindal's hair?

Charley told Mindal to put her shirt back on.

"It has to be a show. We show a little, the tips give. We show a little more, they give more. Have you ever been to a strip club?"

"Once," she said.

"But it was really a pizza place," I said. "We just had to walk through the stripping part to use the bathroom."

She made a face she had refined over years of friendship, the "Stop talking you're ruining it for me" face. It always meant I would keep talking for at least ten more minutes. I needed to be interrupted to stop, maybe even asked to leave.

"Can you go back to the car to get the blueberries?" she said. "We're out in here."

Now they were a we. She was going to sleep with him, and a shared hatred of cock blocking that rivaled our hatred of U.S. foreign policy dictated that I should let her. We had once been virgins for too long. That was why we climbed, so she could sleep with good-looking morons. Mindal insisted on the ways they were smart. They could fix their vans when the vans broke down. They could place gear. But they didn't understand her. Or maybe I didn't understand her. Nobody had infused me with natural antidepressants as a child. Back at the car, I looked for the berries, looked at the pool. I already had on a bikini. We could sneak in later to swim, maybe after we'd filmed ourselves singing folk songs. I suspected I could talk her down to folk songs.

"We're going to make a movie," I said, returning myself to the we fold. "This van is our trailer."

"Yeah!" said Charley. "I like to think of myself as a director."

"We'll make it like a seventies porno!" said Mindal.

"That was a good decade," I told Charley. "We were born."

Mindal made her "Stop talking about how old we are" face. I made my "Too late you shouldn't have brought up the seventies" face.

"Mature women are hot," he said.

"We know more about how to please men and ourselves," I said.

"Young girls, they don't know what they're doing," he said. "That's why I don't sleep with too many of them."

"Do you like girls or boys better?"

I had a new hunch about Charleycumsalot. It was actually an old hunch, a new idea to say something about it.

"Some of the tips get this notion about me that I must be gay because I don't sleep with too many girls."

"And you show them your cock every night," said Mindal. "That might be swaying their opinion."

"Yeah, but the audience is diverse," he said. "I'm sure some of them want to see me with a woman. And an older woman would be great."

"But do you like women?" I said. "Or would it just be to get more tips?"

"I like you two," he said. Charley sat back on a couch that had seen a lot of cum. He patted either side of himself. Neither of us moved. We made the same face.

AT THE LAWYER's a week later, I got an email.

"Charley took mescaline, freaked out. Very bad. Call when L is at lunch."

L was our code for lawyer.

"I thought Charley was sober," I typed back. "L doesn't take a lunch."

L was the last of the Dictaphone generation, or was at least trying to prolong the idea of that generation. He was young enough that he could have learned how to use a computer, and other lawyers found it confusing that he signed every email "Very Truly Yours." The signoff had become a joke between me and L's evening typist, Gray, whose suicide note I'd found open on the screen the day I started the job. Gray stuck around, though, long enough to make edits to his suicide note (it was a living document), and to begin flirting with me using the Very Truly Yours signoff for our intraoffice memos. He had a second job shouting landmarks at tourists from the top of a bus, and a third job tending to a girlfriend who seemed to dress exclusively in period costume. He had typed for L the entire time I was road tripping with Mindal and he was ready to kill me.

"You and Neal Cassady made it back in one piece," he said.

"She's sleeping by the marina," I said. "I'm back in Oakland. I had to kick out my subletter."

"You can't keep doing that. Shit or get off the pot."

"That's what Alexis says about you proposing."

It was nice to see that I still had the office zing in me, the gallows humor of the coffee-brewing class. Gray and I talked about library school the way draft dodgers talked about Canada. L liked to hire well-read people to fetch his coffee. I wrote my name in the books I lent him, in the books I left in Mindal's car, books she could finish in half the time it would take me or L, but which she wouldn't touch if they had my name in them.

Mindal was clear about what belonged to her, what belonged to me. Now she had a high Charley. He was hers. I thought about helping, but what would I do? Hold him till he came down? Hold her while she held him? We could turn on the cam, make an experimental film called "Cumming Down." Humor didn't play well with tips. Nobody wanted a laugh when they were seeking what Charley was stroking. I checked Charley's cam page, his various wish lists. Gifts were a kind of tip. The pictures of what he wanted scared me more than the money. It was hard not to look. L wasn't savvy enough to install one of those net nannies, so I had to nanny myself.

"Please pick up a wisteria salad with extra wisteria," L dictated onto his most recent cassette.

L's wife had him on a diet that involved salads made of edible flowers. She had bulk shipments of vitamins sent to the office, some of which I pilfered for Mindal. I tried to reach my friend while I stood in line for salad.

"Hey comrade, how's tricks?"

"Not good. He's split."

"He drove away in his motor home?"

"No, he took BART. I told him to stay here till the peyote wore off, but he said he needed to see San Francisco. You know he's never been outside of Oregon?"

"I bet he's meeting one of his web johns."

"Oh God. Do you think he uses condoms?"

"No."

"On his cam page, it just says he's bi-curious."

"Mindal."

"Can you get AIDS from pre-cum?"

"We've been over this before. The research is inconclusive."

"Why don't they fund more studies? This is an important issue for idiots who use the withdrawal method."

"I couldn't agree more," I said.

I stopped at a drugstore on my way back to work to buy a box of condoms. I wasn't sure if it was for me or for them. I could give her a few as a token goodbye gift, then use the rest to resume sleeping with the reluctantly urban, sous chefs and wine dealers, cognitive behavioral therapists, divorced pro- grammers with one son. They all had erectile dysfunction.

"Thank you for taking me with you into the world," I would write on L's letterhead. "Please be safe. I'm staying here."

Or I could get back in the car with her, convince her to ditch Charley. There would be other Charleys, though, Charleys after Charleys, miles of Charleys, long stretches of highway sponsored by Charley.

I left the salad in front of my boss, trying not to interrupt what looked like a stream-of-consciousness Motion to Dismiss. Inspiration struck him legally. I liked having no idea what was going on. Somewhere in my gourmet suburb, they had been preparing us for L's career, for file folders and logic you could monetize. I had done all the work as a means to no end. L looked up, waved me away. "You'll hear this all later," was the message. "I don't want to spoil it for you."

I sat down to a pile of folders and a tape, a time capsule from the last half hour. L got a lot done by not taking a lunch. The work ethic was alive and well in America. Some people spent their lunch hour whoring. Others fetched lunches for people not taking lunches. Lunch kept the city employed, an entire industry of boxed salads and rubber-banded soups. Mindal would say we had been separated from the land, from grow- ing our own soup. I agreed, but I didn't want to plow. Farmers from our socioeconomic bracket usually lasted a season before returning to the city with phone memories full of radish pics. I was hungry. Men like L could subsist on flowers. He would live forever in the absence of a moral compass. I was going to die young, not from falling off a rock, not from melanoma, but from something grayer that I couldn't yet name.

Write What You Know

I ONLY KNOW about parent death and sluttiness. What else do I know? I know about the psychology of Jewish people who have assimilated, who dye their hair, who worry about bizarrely specific allergies: Does the Mee Grob have soy sauce? The Mee Grob is fine. Melissa had it last time and she was fine.

I know about liberal guilt and sexual guilt and taking liberties sexually, even though I haven't actually done any of the liberties I know about, except once something with a very small dildo, it hardly counts. I know about unrequited love, and once love that was requited, but not for very long. I know about baseball—it didn't take that long to learn it. I know about relief pitchers, and which guy switch hits. When guys know other guys, they know something I'm left out of. Guys know about towels—towels are a big part of how they know each other, in the locker rooms where they only use each other's last names. The first name is what the girlfriend calls them, when she calls them. She's got a ponytail, she's got boots, she's got chlamydia. No, she doesn't got chlamydia. She's got a mom and a dad and a bathroom at home with a rug on the toilet seat. She's got a ponytail.

I don't know about the rug on the toilet seat. Jewish people who have assimilated rarely keep rugs there. They won't hang a flag. They will get a tiny Christmas tree with irony, or a bigger Christmas tree if they are more serious about assimilating and less serious about irony. I know a girl whose parents ruined her. They had a tree. They even had a wreath. My friend knew how to play the piano, and how not to eat any meal except breakfast, and eventually she knew how to trade stocks, and then how to give up trading to start a food blog for former anorexics, with recipes, and then I didn't know her anymore.

I know how to lose a friend for not caring enough about Unitarian Universalism, and how to lose a friend for not attending her adult bat mitzvah, and how to lose a friend for telling her to dump her Catholic boyfriend, not because I abhor Catholicism or think it is the worst religion, but because he is dumb. I know how to get that friend back by telling her it's none of my business if she wants to marry a dumb man—leaving out the word "dumb"—to get her back by apologizing for pretending to know things I can't know, saying that only the two people inside a thing can know how dumb each other are, to get her back by waiting until she knows what I know, and I can stop pretending I don't.

Acknowledgments

I wish to acknowledge the editors who first published these stories: Carla Blumenkrantz, Keith Gessen, Ben Kunkel, Ben Marcus, Halimah Marcus, Lynne Tillman, and Rebecca Wolff. Thanks to my book's editor, Diana Miller, for her patience and insight, to Sonny Mehta, and to everyone at Knopf. Thanks to my agent, Peter Straus. Thanks to Jackie Delamatre, Andrea Donnelly, Nora Friedman, Patrick Gallagher, Tom Grosheider, George Loh, Kara Levy, Sam Lipsyte, José Miguel Palacios, Lilah Ringler, Rachel Schiff, Freida Schiff, Erika Scott, Rachel Sherman, Tom Drury, Alex Waxman, and Emily Meg Weinstein. I couldn't have done it without you. Thanks to the MacDowell Colony. Thanks finally to my dad, who loved books and taught me to love them.

Also published by
JM Originals in 2016

Blind Water Pass
by Anna Metcalfe

Anna Metcalfe's stories are about communication
and miscommunication – between characters and
across cultures. Whether about a blithely entitled
English teacher in a poor Beijing school, an immigrant
female taxi driver in Paris, or a young Chinese girl
spouting made-up Confucian phrases to please tourists,
the stories examine the assumptions we make about
other people, and about ourselves.

Blind Water Pass is an auspicious debut by
a superb young writer.

Also published by
JM Originals in 2016

Marlow's Landing
by Toby Vieira

*Call this a river. You had to be insane to go
diving in it, or desperate, or both.*

Marlow's Landing is a dangerous place. It's days
up-river. There are huts, and some men with guns,
and a very big pink stone. What the hell is an
accountant from Hull doing there?

Marlow's Landing is a story of our world; a deadly
place of double-crossing and diamond dealing, of
smugglers and jungle madness. And it's the story of
Goldhagen, a man who gets what he wants.